"Balzan drew back, caught the lunger to his right, and gutted the soldier, who collapsed with a horrified shriek.

"It was always the same. Blood, screaming and death. Balzan was sickened by the carnage he inflicted. Yet it was not of his choosing. So why? In a world made up of so many continents, why did creature take the sword to creature? Whatever the choice between reason and destruction, they never met—the sword was always victorious over the tongue.

'Savagery always commanded reason, and power dictated to logic.' Balzan plunged his sword into another Krell . . ."

THE
LIGHTS
OF ZETAR

Wallace Moore

PYRAMID BOOKS ▲ NEW YORK

THE LIGHTS OF ZETAR
A PYRAMID BOOK

Produced by Lyle Kenyon Engel

Copyright © 1975 by Lyle Kenyon Engel

Pyramid edition published September 1975
Second printing, February 1976

ISBN: 0-515-03934-9

Library of Congress Catalog Card Number: 75-15480

Printed in the United States of America

———————————————————————

Pyramid Books are published by Pyramid Communications, Inc.
Its trademarks, consisting of the word "Pyramid" and the por-
trayal of a pyramid, are registered in the United States Patent
Office.

PYRAMID COMMUNICATIONS
(Harcourt Brace Jovanovich)
757 Third Avenue, New York, N.Y. 10017

Chapter One

The morath, with wings furled and reptilian tail curled around its clawed feet, shifted its weird humanoid head and focused its eyes on the human before it. Never before had it seen such a creature, a tall thing with two arms and two legs and a head growing between its shoulders. It was hairless, except for the shoulder-length brown locks that were tied with a length of silver cord. The alien here was the two-legged youth who stood before the morath. He had originally come from a planet known as Earth. It was the third planet from the sun in the faraway solar system. Now he was a prisoner in a world in which he did not belong: a planet that was twice the size of Earth, a world with two moons and many different races. The alien had never known his parents. He had been adopted by the Cat People who had rescued him from his parents' spacecraft. The Cat People had named him Balzan; his first twenty years of life had been spent in their society. All this had ended a year before when his village had been destroyed by the Albs, a reptilian race; since then Balzan had become a wanderer in a savage world of the survival of the fittest.

The creature's red tongue snaked out at the human with the pink skin and futile bravery. The morath hissed and its sound reached thunderous proportions. Its torso rippled and heaved and, from the fanged face, its large eyes glowered.

Balzan held the Kharmite sword that had served him so well and faced the creature into whose lair he had stumbled. His muscles gleamed under the sun as he watched to see what the behemoth would do.

The beast leaned back on its haunches and cocked its head to one side as it seemed to cautiously scrutinize the

5

pink-skinned object it had snared. Then, it stamped its hooves madly and approached closer.

Balzan knew that this was not a herbivore, but a carnivorous beast with a blood lust that would only be satisfied by his own death.

The human attacked first. Dashing forward with sword raised, he crouched and rolled beneath the creature and slashed at the rear legs.

The sword bit deep and blood spurted freely. With a scream of startled pain, the morath collapsed backward. Its great wings flailed the air, and it bellowed in agonized rage. Balzan saw that its stomach was not hard reptilian skin, armor-like and practically impenetrable, but was soft and covered only by a thin layer of brownish fur.

The morath roared and regained its stance. The human had drawn first blood and therefore found new depths of boldness. He approached the beast from the rear just as it reeled to face him.

Balzan backed away slightly as the enraged morath charged clumsily. Suddenly he found himself sprawled flat on his back. He had tripped over a lopar bush behind him and its thorns had cut into his calves like razors when he fell.

The morath reared, its hooves flashing above Balzan's head. For an instant the prime target was clear and open—the soft underbelly of the creature. The sword plunged deep into the reptilian flesh. Globs of rich black blood trickled out over the sword and onto Balzan's hands. The creature screamed and staggered back.

Balzan rolled to a safe distance from the beast and saw it double in pain, its talons grasping at its midsection. While the morath roared in agony, Balzan leaped upon it and thrust his sword deep into the neck and shoulders of the roaring beast which had one claw clutching at its stomach while the other was reaching for the human.

Balzan now circled the beast, lunging and cutting at the feet. The morath, spraying droplets of black blood in all directions, rose on its hind legs and staggered backward. Overcome by the massive slashes of the blade, the beast twisted, stiffened, and fell heavily.

Balzan stood grim faced over the morath and wiped his blood-stained sword over its wings. He took off his hide tunic, now covered with blood, and tossed it savagely to the

6

ground. He had not wished to kill the creature, yet it seemed that wherever he trod on the planet, death always followed.

* * *

Balzan was a youth in a world in which he did not belong or care to belong. Since the time he could remember he had always been regarded as a freak. He had been treated kindly by the Cat People, but there was always the undercurrent of disgust or, even worse, pity, because he was different. Still, he longed for the Cat People who had been his only family. Even more, he wanted kinship with his own kind. This he knew was impossible, so he became a loner. He was Balzan of Endore, who wandered aimlessly in search of a home, a direction, a purpose.

His greatest concern was the fear of never finding his destiny. There were many races and creatures in this world he now trod, but he was unique. He was the alien. He was powerful and intelligent enough to combat any threat or adversary except one—loneliness.

Balzan had realized when he was five years old that he was different, that his features were hairless except for his head and genitals, and that in no way did he resemble the Endorians, bipeds who resembled Earth cats.

His education began when Lomar, his adopted father, took him to the spacecraft in which his parents had died. His teacher was a metallic-voiced ship's computer that tutored him in his studies as the years passed.

His parents had been Weldon and Katherine Rice, both scientists and pilots of the smashed spaceship. They had been on a mission during the twenty-sixth century on Earth and had been caught in a space transference which had whisked them from the solar system to this world that was now Balzan's home.

His name was Paul Brian Rice and he had survived only because he had been sleeping in stasis within a safety cube.

Lomar adopted him and named the Earth-child Balzan, after a hero of the Cat People. He taught the child all he knew of the ways of the world.

Slowly, painstakingly, Balzan had learned of his origins and of his parents' death. The teacher in the spacecraft furthered his education and soon Balzan knew that he might

7

be forever doomed to remain on a planet without any of his own kind to turn to for solace or for love.

It was when the Albs destroyed the Endorian village with their terrible neutron swords and took hostages that Balzan had begun his trek.*

* * *

He replaced his tunic and sheathed his sword. His only other possession was his therb, an Endorian weapon designed by the Cat People. It was a whip with a handle containing a virulent poison and a barbed tip that discharged the poison upon contact.

The sky was now pale green and soon the first of the two moons would appear. The land would be bathed in a chameleon blanket soon, colors changing as the day grew faint. Yet the lowland he trod was pleasant and he saw there was an abundance of thoral fruit trees in the distance preempting all other thoughts except nourishment. Balzan walked wearily toward the dense forest ahead.

* * *

The sweet fruit tasted like fine Uran wine to Balzan who was famished and fatigued after his battle with the morath. If the creature had been a herbivore, Balzan would have dined on roasted flesh instead, but since the animal had been carnivorous the meat would have been revolting. His hunger appeased, he trod on into the gathering gloom of the black branches that screened the sky from his view.

Presently he entered a clearing where he came upon the crumbling remains of what might have been a nested temple, complete with battered artifacts. Around the structure were patches of low thorny vegetation. Balzan saw nothing uncommon in this; the planet was strewn with ruins about which little was known.

The structure looked as if it had been abandoned for centuries, yet something stirred in Balzan that he could not pinpoint. The air was too quiet, nothing seemed to move; it was as if he had suddenly entered a vacuum.

He started to enter the archway leading to the temple. At

* See Balzan #1—*The Blood Stones*

the same instant, the air was split by a full-throated shriek of horror. For a moment Balzan had the impression that the sound surrounded him. Then another scream ripped the silence and Balzan realized that it was that of a female voice.

Balzan, out of reflex, drew his sword and leaped from the archway back into the clearing, his eyes darting in every direction. From the brush came a movement and then a humanoid female came staggering into view clutching her side.

She resembled the Kharnites in a way, except that she was much smaller in stature and had the same hair coloring as Balzan. She saw him and her lips parted to form a word, then there was a sucking sound and a blast of wind.

Balzan shielded his eyes for an instant, then he saw the woman fall face down as she let out a gasp and lie motionless. Balzan dropped beside the body. He gently turned the head to one side, grunted, and then turned the body completely over.

Her face was covered with small, ringlike, red blotches that were fading slowly. Balzan saw that she was clutching an object tightly in her fist. He forced it open. In it was a twisted, scabrous-looking object of no particular color; it looked like a mummified finger. It also looked as though part of it had been eaten away.

His face impassive, Balzan rose and glanced about him. He thought he caught a movement in the brush beside him, but, on investigating, he found nothing. Something had killed the woman who was lying before him, and not in a very pleasant way. Yet, what death was pleasant?

How had the computer teacher described it to him in those years of instruction in the abandoned spaceship? "Hostility and love are interrelated to the extent that emotional fiber exists, and as it exists it locks both into a vulnerable position. Sometimes death is the catalyst. War is not the only scourger, nor hunger, but greed, passion, and hatred."

So absorbed in his thoughts was he that Balzan did not realize he was no longer alone. He heard a sound and turned rigidly, his eyes opening wide with amazement. Balzan, as if hypnotized, stared at the sight before him. Then, without the slightest warning, there was a hurricane of motion. Balzan had a brief impression of a blocky body, man-sized but not the least like a man, and of tentacles reaching for his face. Then there was the blast of the sucking sound again and he fell.

The creature was upon him in an instant. He smashed his fist into the side of its ugly head and it rolled off him. It attempted to rise and Balzan's foot shot out and struck it in the head. He heard a snap and the creature slumped and then rolled back onto its side.

He was on his feet in an instant. Out of the corner of his eye he saw that several man-shaped creatures had slipped soundlessly from the brush. To the youth they looked almost human: lean men, with almond-colored faces, dressed in tunics which bore what looked like a military emblem. The severe jutting of their foreheads was the only thing that made them appear grotesque. In the forefront of the group, a man who seemed to be the commander eyed Balzan with obvious disgust.

Balzan counted six of them and noted that they were holding what looked like weapons resembling Kharnite electropads, only more sophisticated.

Balzan's attention focused almost at once on the commander. His tunic was white and, oddly, less decorated than the others. Even more importantly, his build, stance, reeked of authority.

Balzan slowly raised his hand and sheathed his sword. "I'm a friend," he said, even though he doubted they shared a mutual language.

The humanoids took no overt notice of the remark or the gesture. Balzan jerked the therb forward, unsnapping the whip from its handle. It flipped out and he flailed it to its full length of forty feet as the men cautiously approached him.

The commander motioned to his men and they separated several paces and began moving again.

"I'm a friend," Balzan repeated, "don't make me kill you."

"You already killed our tracker," the commander answered in a voice without emotion.

Balzan was amazed that they spoke a common language and a wide smile came to his lips. "The creature attacked me. I was only defending myself. We speak as one, can we not talk of this without violence?"

The commander raised his arm and the men stopped. He

eyed Balzan for a moment and then spoke slowly and deliberately.

"For an Orathian, you appear unusually intelligent. Explain."

"Orathian?" Balzan echoed.

"You deny you worship their god?"

"What is an Orathian?"

"Don't try to be clever."

"I said," Balzan was issuing each syllable like a bullet, "what is an Orathian?"

The commander drew a deep breath. "The only other race that speaks our tongue is the Orathian. Do you deny that you are conversing with me at this very moment?"

"I don't deny that I'm conversing with you. In fact, I'm very happy that I am. However, I am not an Orathian."

"You appear to be a very convincing liar, whatever religion you practice."

"Listen, I apologize for killing your tracker, but it attacked me and if your beast killed that woman, then it should be you apologizing."

The commander sneered. "Your apology doesn't satisfy me for an instant. However, you do intrigue me, since you claim you are not an Orathian and yet you understand our language. I must admit there is a difference about you. Still, you are our prisoner and must accompany us to the Monitor."

"Wait a minute," Balzan said icily, "we appear to be somewhat of the same race, but we are not. I am alien to this world and therefore am not an Orathian. I am Balzan of Endore and I go nowhere that I do not choose."

"We will soon change that bit of philosophy," the commander smirked.

Balzan lifted a hand to them. "If you wish to die then come. If you cannot accept me as a friend, then you damn sure will know me as an enemy."

In the brief silence that followed, Balzan became aware that two of the soldiers had moved to his extreme right, three to his left, leaving only the commander in front of him.

"Don't fence with me, Orathian, this is merely a ruse to delay us. As for a test of strength you are outnumbered six to one. You have come out of the neutral zone and thus have challenged us. Because of this you and your inferior

11

race will pay with enough slaughter and destruction so that you will not ignore our laws again."

Balzan scoffed at the commander. "You sound like the Albs, blowing your trumpet, but not knowing who your master is."

"The Krells have no masters," the commander snapped, "but we do possess many slaves and, among them, you Orathians number in the thousands."

"For the last time I am not an Orathian," Balzan snapped.

"The language and visual evidence weigh heavily against you."

"Then I guess you'll have to die in your ignorance," Balzan said.

"A distinct possibility," the commander agreed, "which only time will prove."

For a moment nothing happened, but the fury that flared between the combatants could not be suppressed. With a savage gesture, the commander motioned his men into action.

The therb cracked; a soldier staggered back and grasped his neck where the barb had torn. Balzan snapped the therb again and it struck another soldier who shrieked with pain and fell.

A soldier leaped on Balzan from behind and both fell to the ground. The soldier stiffened suddenly and rolled off Balzan, a knife hilt protruding beneath his sternum.

Balzan rolled to his feet and grabbed his sword and swung it in an arc that sliced through two of the Krells, dropping them instantly. Their entrails spilled from the gaping wounds across their chests and stomachs.

The commander darted at him swinging his baton. Twisting and bringing his sword up, Balzan parried the Krell's blow and, with a swift kick to the commander's groin, sent him sprawling backward.

Balzan drew back, caught the lunger to his right, and gutted the soldier who collapsed with a horrified shriek.

It was always the same—blood, screaming, and death. Balzan was sickened at the carnage he inflicted. Yet, it was not of his choosing. Why, in a world made up of so many continents, did creature take the sword to creature? Was the life cycle so insignificant? Whatever the choice between reason and destruction, they never met, the sword was al-

12

ways victorious over the tongue. Savagery always commanded reason, and power dictated to logic.

Balzan plunged his sword into another Krell and drew back. The commander attacked him now with a vengeance. He avoided each thrust and answered it with one of his own. He stopped the momentum of the blade. With a jerk he pulled the commander to him and smashed his fist into his nose, sending him reeling. The commander staggered, then charged again. Balzan leaped into the air and his foot caught the Krell in the throat. The commander's face registered shock, then, gasping for breath, he slumped to his knees.

Another soldier attacked and Balzan ended his life with two quick thrusts into the abdomen and neck. As swiftly as it began, it was over. Now five dead Krells lay at Balzan's feet. Their commander, struggling for breath, could only muster a weak motion of surrender before he collapsed into unconsciousness.

Chapter Two

The comet Ria, described by Lomar as the fleetest of burning brilliance, shot into the sky. As in a dream a new face changed the planet's surface. It was the sight that Balzan had always wondered at these past two decades. It was always the same music to the eye of the beholder. Two moons resplendent in the heavens; where one had been now there were two.

They were conflicting in color and altered the terrain. The brilliant one, stately, majestic, almost stationary, shed its steady light upon the world below. The paler moon, flecked with particles of ebony and scarlet, stood as a great and glorious orb to its sister moon. They complemented each other in contrast.

They appeared so low they seemed to graze the treetops, a gorgeous spectacle that held the youth beneath the spell of its enchantment as it always had.

"The light that shelters and cheers me," murmured Balzan of Endore. The youth sighed and let his gaze fall again to the stern realities beneath. The dead Krells that lay at his feet only provoked anger in Balzan. They could have elected to receive him in friendship and live. Instead, they chose to die.

A wind stirred. The trees moved in restless circles as the cool air refreshed Balzan now that his fury had abated. The youth replaced his weapons and once again moved out into the silence of the forest, leaving the scene of his carnage behind him.

Balzan trod through the night—he was troubled. Who were the Krells? The Orathians? And, if they were humanoids as he, why were they in conflict?

As Balzan crept over the brow of a hill down toward a

14

valley, his presence was hidden by the darkness of the night from the view of any chance predator or Krell that might be in the area. The larger moon was just shifting now to begin its leisurely journey through the heavens. Balzan hoped to find water and food, gain distance from the Krells, and, if fortunate, sleep.

He came to thick foliage at the base of the valley. Sometimes he stumbled, for the shadows cast by the twin moons were distorted and gave illusions of depth where none existed. Balzan knew that he would come upon water soon and where water was abundant, there would be fruit-bearing trees. Out of the thick grass Balzan saw the stream ahead.

He drank slowly, but deeply. He bathed his face and hands. Next he sought out the fruit of the trees adjacent to the stream. They were edible berries that could be eaten raw. They were overly sweet and left an aftertaste in Balzan's mouth.

Occasionally he returned to the stream to drink, each time moderately. Always were his eyes and ears alert for the first signs of danger, but he had neither seen nor heard anything to alarm him.

Presently the thirst and hunger were satisfied. Balzan prepared to move on. He filled the pocket of his hide tunic with berries. He was reluctant to leave the water for he was afraid it could be a long time before he found water again. He had nothing in which to carry water, so he would have to content himself with the berries he had gathered.

After a last drink at the stream, he rose and eyed the valley ahead. But, even as he did so, he became suddenly tense with apprehension. He could have sworn something moved in the shadows beneath a tree ahead of him.

For a long moment Balzan did not move or breathe. His eyes remained fixed upon the dense shadows below the tree, his ears straining through the silence of the night.

Something was hiding in the shadows. With a reflex action he unsnapped the therb and squinted into the darkness. It was the strain of uncertainty that weighed upon him. He cast quickly about him in search of refuge, should the thing prove dangerous.

A moan came from the trees beyond. Balzan recognized the sound, the lone whine of a hunting carnivore, but it seemed far in the distance. Something was a lot closer to him in the shadows, but what?

Slowly, and without taking his eyes from the shadows of the tree, he moved toward the overhanging branches. He was halted by a female voice uttering an almost shrieking wail.

"Master, please spare me."

Balzan's eyes searched the blackness but could see nothing. "Show yourself."

A woman emerged from the gloom. Obviously, she was an Orathian, since she resembled the slain woman and had the same hair coloring. She was younger and her eyes held the contrasting colors of green and gold. Other than that, her coloring and body were the same as Balzan's. In her outstretched hand she held a mummified finger like the older woman had held, as if to offer it in tribute.

"Who are you?" Balzan snapped.

The woman, with her head bowed and still extending the hideous-looking object, spoke softly.

"I am Tarlene of the house of Rashton. I offer my tribute to you, mighty Krell, and implore mercy upon my worthless life."

Her body was sheathed in a hide tunic as Balzan's was. Yet he saw that she was lithe and beautiful. Her black hair fell freely to her shoulders.

"I am no Krell," Balzan told her softly, "and whatever that thing is in your hand, you can keep it."

Tarlene let her gaze slowly come up and rest on Balzan's face. Her eyes smiled, yet she still trembled.

"If you are not a Krell, Master, what god are you?"

Balzan chuckled. "If my sister Kitta could hear you she would roar with laughter at that. I am no god. I am Balzan of Endore."

"I have no knowledge of Endore, Master."

"It is a land far from here. It is a land of the past so do not concern yourself. But why are you concealed here in the darkness?"

The woman stiffened visibly. "My mother and I left the Neutral Zone to pay homage at our temple."

"Temple?"

"Yes. The Krell masters have dictated that we no longer may have our periods of tribute."

"Yet you defied them."

"Yes. My mother was with coming child and we risked our lives to present our god with the Stayks."

16

"What are Stayks?"

"The finger of the Staykton is revered by our god. It is a beast we herded once for ourselves, now for the Krells."

Balzan replaced his therb and scrutinized the woman. "Your mother is dead. She was killed by the Krell beast they use as a tracker."

"I am aware. I heard her screams. She is with our god now and is content. He knews she died in tribute to his glory."

"You don't seem to care much, do you?" Balzan asked.

"The dictates of the Krell are not for inferiors to question, Master," the woman replied softly.

"I am not your Master," Balzan snapped. "I am Balzan and we are both people, not animals. Man is neither a slave nor a master."

"You have great weapons," Tarlene said, indicating his sword and therb.

"I use them for protection. I killed the Krells that killed your mother, but only because I was forced to do so."

The woman drew herself up to her full height. "I am indebted to you, Balzan of Endore," she said without emotion.

Balzan smiled. "You owe me nothing. Now if you will lead the way, I will return you safely to your people."

Tarlene raised her slim brows. "We cannot journey to my people at night, not with the beasts that roam the forest. We must take shelter in the trees until dawn."

Balzan knew only too well the carnivores that preyed at night. He agreed with the woman. "All right, this tree is as good as any."

Balzan then swung nimbly to the lower branches and assisted Tarlene. As she felt his muscular arms pull her to him she felt safe and secure. The strange youth was strong and fearless to her, a complete opposite to the men who called themselves Orathian warriors—warriors who cowered and knelt at the heels of their Krell masters.

Balzan and Tarlene huddled together in the crook of the tree. The wail of a distant carnivore split the night air at regular intervals. The woman clung to the tree in desperation. As she dozed Balzan saved her from falling. Now the night air grew cold and she shivered. Balzan cradled the woman in his arms to warm and soothe her. She looked at him with her beautiful eyes and once again slept.

The night wore on, interlaced with wails of carnivores and screams of the smaller animal life that had fallen prey to their night stalking.

Then the sun and both moons rode together in the sky, blending their beauty and mystery to create a strange but beautiful dawn.

They set out for Tarlene's village. In the morning light, with the sun dancing upon her hair, she was even more beautiful, Balzan thought. As they made their way into the valley she told him of her people and the Krells who had become their masters.

"Why do your people let the Krells enslave you? Do you have no warriors among your numbers?"

"My people have not practiced the art of war for decades. The Krells possess weapons that are frightening to behold."

Balzan remembered the silver baton the Krell commander had wielded. He had been powerless against Balzan. The weapon carried a suggestion of splendid craftsmanship, but had been of rather poor utility against the therb. "In what way do you serve the Krells, Tarlene?"

The woman smiled. "We are forced to serve them in any way they desire. The males of our race toil beneath the ground in their mines. The women and children are utilized mostly in domestic service. If one of our numbers pleases a Krell citizen we are taken as a body servant."

Balzan listened and was amazed at how close the Krell civilization paralleled the Kharnite race. The only difference was that the Krells were completely humanoid with the exception of their almond-colored skin and jutting foreheads.

"Our village is surrounded by predatory enemies. We are the herdsmen for the Krells' Stayktons. We are fortunate in a sense, since none in my village, as yet, has been condemned to the mines. There is a constant need of workers for the mines. Many other Orathian villages have not been so fortunate."

"Then the Krells are a race of warriors?" Balzan asked.

"Yes. Although the Krell citizens are taxed heavily by Androth, our Supreme Master, they still avoid the mines. The need for many slaves seems to be in Androth's constant working of the mines. The citizens must either furnish him slaves or do the work themselves. Of course, they would not consider the latter."

"So your people are the instruments of the Krells' labor?"

"I suppose that is our purpose, Master," she replied shyly.

"Balzan," he corrected.

"Balzan."

"How many villages of your people exist?"

"Countless. The Krells have a large empire and wherever their sky ships journey, slaves are found. The Orathians are not the only servants."

"Are there any Krells in your village?"

"No. We see them only on daily patrols and once a month when we herd their beasts to the city."

"The city?"

"Manator. The city of the Krells," she announced with a hint of pride in her voice.

Balzan shook his head in dismay. Tarlene, seeing this, looked puzzled. "What is it? Did I say something that was offensive to you, Master?"

Balzan controlled his anger as he spoke. "I told you, don't call me master again. You did not offend me, Tarlene. I just find it hard to understand that you accept your bondage so calmly . . . even proudly."

The woman smiled. "This has been my way of life. I certainly would not change places with the Gorans."

"Gorans?"

"They are also slaves of the Krells, but they are used in a more terrible manner. They are bred just to feed the Krells' pets."

"Pets?"

"Yes, every Krell master has a certain number of pets and the Gorans are used to feed them."

Balzan shuddered. The woman related this to him in the same nonchalant manner she took the death of her mother. It was apparent the Krells not only kept the Orathians enslaved physically but also had succeeded in removing any semblance of willpower as well. The woman was almost content in her situation and this troubled Balzan.

Passive resistance was one of the few traits of creatures that Balzan could not comprehend. The Cat People had always taught him to fight and to defend himself. Their teachings always remained. He remembered the day his adopted father died. He saw again the fire that had engulfed Lomar's shroud-covered body, and a part of him had died as well. He blamed himself for not being in the village when it had been attacked.

Tarlene saw that he was lost in his thoughts and brought him back to the present by gently touching his arm. "You will have a fondness for my village, Balzan, and my people will have a fondness for you as well."

"Are we close to your village?"

"Yes, it is only a short way now. My brother Jem, I am sorry to say, you may find offensive."

"Why is that?"

"He is different. He hates our masters and I fear will have great difficulty in the future."

Balzan smiled inwardly. Her brother would probably be the only Orathian he would have a fondness for. He reached into his tunic and pulled out the Krell silver baton he had taken from the commander. Upon seeing this, Tarléne stopped walking and collapsed at his feet. Her hands were turned upright into a position of subservience; her features were instantly transformed into a mask of fear.

Tears crowded her eyes and she practically screamed at Balzan. "Master, I, Tarlene, do accept the Monitor as my Confessor, the Krells as my divine masters and protectors. I beseech you to discipline me for my act of defiance. I was led to this by my mother's evil and insanity. Spare me though, the kiss of the caron."

The silver baton he held was obviously the "caron." If it wielded such power and instilled such terror, why had he defeated it with the simple Endorian therb? He reached down and roughly brought Tarlene to her feet. His words were overly brutal. "You disgust me. Do you think every man you see is a torturer of women? What is this thing and why are you so terrified?"

The woman attempted to fall to her knees again, but Balzan held her. She began sobbing and soon reached hysteria. "Master . . . I beseech . . ."

Balzan's open palm struck her across the face twice, in rapid succession.

She fought to control herself, but her words still were racked with sobs.

"Don't . . . use it . . . please."

"I won't, Tarlene, believe me," Balzan said, trying to soothe the terrified woman. "I only wanted to ask you what it was. I took it from the Krells."

"It . . . is . . . the caron. . . ."

"Yes. I know what you call it, but how does it function?"

"It causes unbearable pain when it is placed upon the skin."

Balzan peered into her eyes, eyes that showed him for the first time in his young life the full measure of terror. Then he touched the baton to his forearm. He felt nothing. He experienced no pain.

The woman looked at him in utter amazement. "You . . . felt . . . nothing. You truly are a god."

"I'm no god and this is nothing but a silver rod. Here, feel it."

The woman leaped back, more hysterical than before. "No—please—"

Balzan saw that the baton, upon sight, had completely transformed the beautiful Orathian into a groveling, incoherent, and pathetic sight. He realized in an instant that the caron wielded no powers, that the Krells had conditioned the Orathians, by some mental process, to react in the manner she had. They had successfully ingrained in her subconscious that the touch of the instrument brought unbearable pain. Balzan also saw that with its appearance, total and almost maniacal loyalty resulted.

He was most curious to see what kind of power demanded that total devotion and fear. He replaced the caron in his tunic and gently lifted the sobbing Tarlene once again to her feet.

"Forgive me, I did not know that the weapon was so powerful. I will not bring it out again. Please, I am sorry."

She could not form her words, but nodded and smiled in relief. A short time later they resumed their journey.

On the fringe of Tarlene's village, Balzan was halted in his tracks by the sight before him. A tower that seemed to climb into the sky loomed in the distance.

"What in the name . . . what is that?" Balzan rasped.

Tarlene, composed now, spoke once again with pride in her voice. "That is the palace of our Governor."

"Is he a Krell?"

"Yes, he governs Orathia for Androth, our Supreme Master. His wife is Androth's own daughter. The Krell city lies far beyond the pinnacles, so Androth appoints a governor for each province in his empire. Chalak is a kind man, he only leaves his palace to inspect our province once a month. The rest of the time he leaves us in peace."

Balzan frowned. "Does a slave really ever have peace, Tarlene, as long as his spirit is in bondage?"

Tarlene looked at the strange youth before her. Suddenly, for the first time in her young life, she could not find words to answer.

* * *

Lenor, the Krell princess, lay on a recliner of soft silk and fur next to a gleaming pool of scented water in a marble basin. Her face was flawless; her carriage, physical perfection. Her almond skin was soft and lovely and her body was graceful in the effortless harmony of her seductive movements. Her hair was coiffured with gold and jewels and precious emeralds from Arakam. Her revealing silk gown, flowing from the winds that entered the apartment from the high altitude, made her a feast for the eyes.

Chalak, her husband, stood staring out of the glass-encased tower at the valley below. He wore the gorgeous trappings of a Krell general. His leather tunic had ornaments and designs of gold embossed on it. His belt was encrusted with silver and diamonds, as were the scabbards of his sword and the ornate holster that held his caron. As he moved through the sunlit room that was laden with plant life and flowers, the rays of his gems enveloped him in a light that was brilliant to the eye. His handsome face was covered with a scowl as he strode across the white marble floor to his wife's recliner.

Lenor regarded him with mute dispassion as he loomed over her. "Give me some wine," he said with a touch of ice in his voice.

Lenor rose from the recliner, stretched her lithe body languidly, and crossed toward the center of the room, where a decanter of wine and silver goblets sat upon a large table. Filling one of the goblets to the brim, she handed it to her husband.

She returned to the comforts of her recliner and eased herself upon it with a feline grace. Chalak drained half of the goblet's contents and his eyes focused on his wife.

22

"You should drink water, my husband. Wine only increases the thirst."

"I enjoy it," he replied, finishing the remainder of his goblet. He slumped beside her and stared at the pool, seeing nothing.

"Orathia. A fine wedding present your father gave me," he said with sarcasm in his words.

Lenor smiled placatingly at him.

"My dear Chalak, it has been said that whoever can rule Orathia can rule Manator as well."

Chalak's eyes brightened as he turned to the woman beside him. "Do you really think that is what Androth has planned for me?"

Lenor smiled wickedly, then tossed her head back and laughed. Her laugh had a full-throated, lyrical quality to it.

"Well?" Chalak demanded.

Lenor touched his arm gently. "I wish I knew my father's mind as well as I know my husband's ambitions."

Chalak leaped to his feet and stared down at her. A sneer curled his lips as he spoke.

"Perhaps you relish your exile in this abode in the clouds, but I do not. I despise it and I despise these imbeciles that I govern. Any common league captain could serve as well."

"Maybe one will be your successor, my husband."

"What do you mean by that?"

"Well, I'm as bored as you are, my dear. Should I ask my father to recall you?"

Chalak stiffened. "You know that would ruin me. Is that what you want?"

Lenor, smiling, answered with amusement in her eyes. "No, my lord, I only wish you to be contented. We will return soon to the city. I promise you."

"How can you promise that?"

"Remember, my dear, the Feast of Zetar comes within a few days and Father will be in retreat. I, his daughter, and you, his general, shall be rulers in his absence."

"Yes, I had forgotten," he said with jubilation in his voice. "Yes, we will return to the city."

"Yes dear, now why don't we try and turn this dreary day into something more pleasant."

Chalak dropped the wine goblet and went to her outstretched arms.

Chapter Three

The Orathian village lay beneath the tower. The forest provided a shelter from the elements. Carnivores hunted at its fringe. Only a small part of the stony ground was cultivated, near the hamlets. Clay and stone huts, roofed with thatch, clustered below the governor's tower.

Herders slept by the beasts in the outer fields, and Stayks crowded the narrow forest trails. Here and there could be seen the white dust and broken stones of a road. A patrol of Krells raised the dust daily, and the men in the fields thronged around to stare at the powerful steeds, the dark cloaks, and the silver batons.

Occasionally, they also were privileged to see the governor's airship gliding placidly over their village. Few Orathians ever saw more than this—except where the roads met at the end of their valley. What lay beyond the hills was unknown and considered hostile. Only a robed chronicler was allowed to journey between villages. The Krells had outlawed tributes to the Orathian gods, but to keep the people tranquil, they did allow their chroniclers to aid and counsel the people in the arts of their old and pagan worship. The Orathians were buried in the valley of their birth without ever having seen any other valley, and they labored without ceasing.

Balzan followed Tarlene into the center of the village. No one came to greet her, it was as if she had never departed. He noticed women working at open hearths. They made their bread with chalk taken from the earth and mixed with flour supplied by the Krell masters.

Balzan saw many old people clustered around the open fires. Their faces were lean, as if they had not the strength to drag themselves about. He saw men digging a pit and several bodies were dragged into it. The entire village had the look of desolation. Balzan noticed only a couple of children and they, like their elders, had the look of hunger upon their small faces.

Tarlene led him to a circle of Orathians who were standing listening to an old man in a black robe who was chanting. With his eyes closed, he had the appearance of an animated corpse.

"It is the Chronicler," Tarlene said, "we are fortunate to find him in our village today."

"Who is the Chronicler?"

"Our holy man, he is stern—I mean, he is in a state of obedience."

Balzan noticed several of the villagers clustering about him. In their hands they held crude wooden weapons that offered no danger to Balzan.

Tarlene burst into the circle of people crowded about the Chronicler.

"Chronicler, I have brought a young god to our village. Please greet him."

Balzan saw the men behind him stop and the group in front of the old man suddenly took the position of obedience. The old man looked at Balzan through milky eyes and his wrinkled face became a mask of fleeting indecision. Then he smiled and approached Balzan. He extended his hands, palms upward.

"I am Taza, the Chronicler. In the name of Orathia, I greet you in peace."

"I am Balzan of Endore," the youth answered, duplicating the old man's motions. "I also greet you in peace."

The Chronicler placed his hand upon the youth's arm. "Let us sit and talk, Balzan of Endore. I have many questions."

"I also have many questions," Balzan answered and followed the old man into one of the thatch huts. He saw Tarlene disappear into the crowd of people without a word of farewell.

The Chronicler motioned to a crude bench. Balzan seated himself and watched the old man study him with intense curiosity.

"I assure you I am not a god," Balzan said, smiling.

The Chronicler nodded and his eyes brightened as he spoke. "Tarlene is a very good child, but she romanticizes and is a little slow. I was aware of the caron in your tunic."

"I am glad that there is one that speaks rationally," Balzan smiled.

"Endore?" the old man scratched at his white beard. "I have never seen that on the empire's maps."

"It is a land far distant from here and is part of no empire," Balzan assured the old man.

"The Krell empire encompasses the world, my son. You are mistaken."

"Until yesterday, I had never heard of a Krell," Balzan answered.

The old man looked completely bewildered. "I am puzzled, my son, you seem as one of us. You speak our common tongue and yet you say you have never heard of your ancestors."

"The Krells or Orathians are not my ancestors. It would be too complicated to explain, so let us just leave it at that."

"And the caron you carry?" The old man pointed to Balzan's tunic and the silver baton protruding from it.

"I took it from a Krell patrol last night. They killed Tarlene's mother and I killed them."

Balzan expected a look of shock or at least a frown to come to the old man's face. He received a smile instead.

"That explains why Tarlene introduced you as a god. Only gods can conquer the Krells."

"You seem amused," Balzan said. "You appear to be more intelligent than the others, yet you, too, are a servant of the Krells."

"I serve, my son, for one reason."

"Yes?" Balzan asked in a mocking tone.

"I have this uncontrollable urge to stay alive. A condition, I hope, that will exist a while longer."

The youth laughed. "Then you can explain a few things to me, old man. To begin with, why did you act so surprised that I had never heard of the Krells?"

"Once again, caution dictates every move I make. For all I knew you could have been an Orathian from a different village spying on us under orders of Chalak."

"Your governor?" Balzan asked.

The Chronicler nodded. "Many of our young men have been recruited for just such a purpose. You do not deny that by appearance you look like an Orathian?"

"No, I don't deny it, but I assure you I am not. Why are

there spies among you? Tarlene led me to believe that the Krells have no opposition."

"There is revolt in the air, my son. You need but to look at this village to see why."

"I know. Yet I cannot understand how a race of people could be so dominated."

"Orathia is but one conquered race in the Krell empire. Our brothers, the Corillians, are also in bondage. I can name you many more races that share our fate. The Krells have weapons that make men cower like children, and the sad thing is that they are harmless weapons that only seem destructive."

"Like the caron?" Balzan offered.

"Yes, a piece of metal that drives our people into muttering idiots. The real danger of the Krells lies in the power of the mind. They have a process developed that completely dominates the will, and it is a very successful one, for we outnumber our masters by three score to one."

Balzan leaned forward and a frown creased his brow. "If you know all this, why haven't you united your people to move against them?"

"How? The sight of the caron, the fear of it, halts any effort I make. You must realize this also, Balzan of Endore, the Krells are a mechanized race, they have air machines, and they possess weapons that *do* kill."

"How many others among you are aware of the Krells' fear-inducers?"

"Many, but those that are cannot gather enough supporters to rally a revolt. I myself advocate a peaceful withdrawal from servitude. There are many young fools that wish to fight with sticks and slings against steel and fire. Ultimately, they will be driven into dust."

"How is it, old man, that your people could be so easily led?"

For a moment the Chronicler seemed about to reply, and Balzan tensed in anticipation; the Chronicler's mouth opened and his lips seemed to quiver. "Hunger can be a terrible thing. The Krells put down our last revolt when I was but a child; many were starved to death. The siege lasted until there was no resistance left. In punishment for that revolt, our period of tribute was abolished and, shortly afterward, the caron was introduced to my people."

He moved closer, and a wrinkled hand came up to touch

27

Balzan's arm. "You must understand, my son, that no man wants to be a slave."

"I do." Then, without hesitation, Balzan offered the Chronicler his hand in friendship. The older man grasped it firmly.

"Come," he said, laboring to his feet, "let us at least provide you with what meager food there is."

After Balzan had eaten and briefly been presented to the village, the two men returned to their discussion. A fire blazed in the hearth.

"The wine is dreadful," Balzan remarked in good humor.

"We ferment it especially for the Krells," the Chronicler laughed. "What are your plans, my son?"

Balzan gazed at the older man and spoke in a sigh. "I really don't have any."

"You would be of great service to my people if you remained."

"I don't understand," Balzan replied.

"Orathia could shed her bonds under a strong leader; a man who can kill six Krells is an asset."

"I killed them in self-defense," Balzan said softly.

The Chronicler gestured his apology. "I did not mean to imply that I was recruiting you as an assassin. I told you I look to a peaceful solution if one exists. Yet, my people are a herd and a herd requires a leader."

"Surely there are men among you who will fight," Balzan interrupted.

"And die," the old man rasped. "The Corillians have been revolting for seven seasons to no avail. Recently we learned that they have resurrected an old machine used centuries ago in warfare, but it has yet to be fired, and I doubt if it ever will."

"I don't know," Balzan said sullenly. "I can't accept the idea that one man alone can help you. I only want to find a place once in my life where there is no war or killing. . . ." His voice trailed off.

The Chronicler was about to reply, but stopped himself before he spoke. He sensed the sudden depression in the younger man and laughed softly.

"That place does not exist, my son, except in our hearts."

"It certainly doesn't here, old man, and that is why I'm leaving."

The old man bowed his head. "Of course, why should

28

you place yourself in jeopardy over a race that disgusts you so much."

"That's not true," Balzan answered, "I can understand superior arms dominating a race. It's just that I . . ."

"Don't belong?" the old man said.

"If you want to put it that way," Balzan said, "yes."

"I see. Do you really belong anywhere?" The Chronicler put out a hand, forestalling Balzan's reply. "You are wandering aimlessly in search of peace and a home. A home is to be made and peace is something that is acquired. My people can be your people, Balzan. I ask not for your life, only your aid. Once Orathia lived in peace and without masters. We could do so again."

The old man studied Balzan's face intently and saw the youth's features relax. "You are a hard man to argue with, but I still don't feel I can be of any help to you," Balzan replied.

"Stay with us a day or so, meet my people, then decide if they are worth your effort."

He watched Balzan a moment longer. At last, he rose and walked slowly out of the hut. Balzan turned and watched him shuffle away. He gazed into the fire and let his thoughts drift to the past, so far and so distant.

He became aware of Tarlene's presence. It had grown dark and she had entered and now she stood beside him. He glanced up at her. Her eyes searched his briefly before she smiled.

"The Chronicler told us you were going to stay," she said.

"For a while," Balzan said. "Sit down beside me." She slipped under his arm and put her head on his shoulder.

"Did you eat?" she asked with concern.

Balzan nodded and fed several small twigs to the fire.

"The Chronicler is very wise, isn't he?" she asked, glancing up at him.

"Yes, very wise."

"But he said you were not a god. You look like a god."

Smiling down at her, Balzan laughed. She frowned and touched his lips. "You still are a god to me."

"And you are a goddess," he said.

"Would you like to kiss me?" she grinned and closed her eyes.

Balzan laughed again, then he kissed her.

Outside the wind freshened and began approaching storm proportions. At the top of the tower that loomed over the village its intensity raged.

Atop the roof of the tower that housed Chalak, the Governor of Orathia, the airship *Razon* tore at its stout moorings. The groaning tackle bespoke the fury of the wind, while the haggard faces of the servants of the visiting dignitary gave evidence of the storm's rage. Only stout lashings prevented the ship from being swept from the tower. The men clung to rails to save themselves from being carried away by each new blast of wind.

Upon the mesh hull of the *Razon* was painted the emblem of Androth, ruler of the Krells. Smaller emblems on colored pennants had been carried away in rapid succession by the storm, just as it seemed to the men watching that the wind would carry the ship itself.

They were amazed that any masts could withstand the force of the wind.

* * *

An hour earlier there had been a visitor to the tower of Chalak. It was Ledan, League Counsel. He had arrived shortly before the storm. He was a bronzed giant of a man. His almond skin was covered only by a military tunic and a counsel's trappings; small dagger and baton were a pleasure to Lenor's eyes. His black hair, steel-gray eyes, and noble features caused the hearts of many Krell women to flutter. Lenor sipped her wine and smiled across at her guest. Chalak stared out at the storm. "It would be foolhardy to attempt to navigate a ship in such a storm. Remain with us till tomorrow, Ledan."

Ledan smiled. "It would be my pleasure, Chalak, as I have military instructions for you from Androth. A day can be spared easily."

"My airship is in the city. I am relieved that it is missing this punishment. These damn towers are ridiculous," Chalak complained.

"But functional," Ledan commented.

Lenor rose and Ledan was instantly on his feet, his head bowed. "Since you have my father's work to be discussed, I shall retire," she said.

The handsome warrior snapped to attention. Lenor gave

Chalak a polite kiss and left the two men with an entourage of servants following at her heels.

"She is beautiful," mused Ledan.

"Yes, I know," replied Chalak indifferently. "But she has changed since I've been at this post. I hate this barren place of misery."

"If you wish to rise in power, Lord Chalak, you must do the difficult."

"Yes, I know," Chalak sneered.

The warrior's face hardened, "Androth is displeased. He wishes to see Orathia made into a more obedient province."

"Yes, I expect he would, but how? The barbarians are impossible."

"In what way?" Ledan asked.

"In their natural resentment of us, they, as a majority, are subservient, but there are rebels everywhere. And then, there's the Chronicler. He goes about placating them, supposedly, but I nurse the feeling he is inciting them."

"Punish them," Ledan snapped.

Chalak smiled broadly and his words were a laugh. "We do, when we can find them."

The warrior refilled his wine goblet and turned to the governor. "You suffer no more than any other Province Governor, you just lack the stamina of enforcement."

"That's ridiculous. I see that the law is obeyed and our King suffers no less tribute. It's just the religion they practice. I tell you they are drunk with it. They believe that some warrior god is coming to deliver them to some type of anti-Krell paradise, and this Chronicler . . ."

"We have heard these rantings before," Ledan interrupted harshly.

"No, this Chronicler is different. He tells these Orathians that their god's power is in every one of them. It is enough to make your head spin."

"There is divinity in only one man . . . our King," Ledan said coldly.

"Yes, I know," Chalak answered, angry at himself for displaying such weakness.

The warrior's mood changed to jubilation. "You've been away too long from the city, Chalak," he said good-humoredly. "Go back to Manator, lay by the sea, forget there is a god in every Orathian."

"That, I would not argue with, except religion seems to be the motivation of these people."

"A touch of the caron will cure that—or perhaps the lash?" Ledan smirked.

Chalak tossed the warrior a look of defiance. "Oh, you can break a man's skull, Ledan, or flog him half to death, but how do you combat what's up here?" He pointed to his forehead. "How do you fight a belief?"

Ledan, amused, set down his wine goblet and walked to the governor's side. "With another belief, Lord Chalak. A belief that if they do not obey and any further revolt occurs, they will be starved to death."

Chalak slumped into a fur-draped chair and sighed. "What are Androth's instructions?"

"The Feast of Zetar begins on the next bilem. You and Princess Lenor will rule while he is in sanctuary. I will serve as your replacement here and implement the new discipline on the Orathians."

Chalak laughed. "I wish you all the luck in the world, my comrade. These savages I bequeath to your loving hands."

Ledan glanced down at the governor and smirked. "Who knows, Lord Chalak, I may accomplish in a short time what you have failed to do in a full revolvement."

"I doubt that, Ledan, but please attempt it. Your ambition only rivals my own. You may begin your terror tactics at your pleasure."

Ledan made a little bow of acquiescence. "Thank you, Lord Chalak, and where would you counsel me to begin?"

"You could start by rooting out the rebels that slaughtered my patrol last night. A full cohort."

The warrior looked shocked. "You lost a commander and five warriors?"

This time it was Chalak's turn to smirk. "What is it, Ledan? Are you afraid there are some men out there that are not afraid of your little silver baton and that you may have to exert a little stamina?"

Ledan's face hardened. "Their corpses will be awaiting your return, Lord Chalak."

"Really?" Chalak smiled. "Do you consider yourself that invulnerable that you can defeat all the rabble of Orathia?"

"I care not for numbers, only in odds, and our odds are always greater than theirs."

"Because we are warriors?" Chalak purred.

"No, because we are Krells."

"Come, let us drink to your instant discovery of the assassins."

The two men toasted each other and drained their goblets.

Ledan strode to the window and stared down at the windswept village below. "Tomorrow," he thought to himself, "you will pay for the slain Krells tenfold. Ten to one, the difference between a Krell and an Orathian."

Chapter Four

Balzan was jarred from his sleep by Tarlene's terrified scream. He leaped to his feet. For an instant he forgot where he was and shook his head in a daze. He looked up to see that the room was full of Krells.

Six armed men ranged the walls, swords and carons gleaming in their hands. The leader, whom Balzan recognized by his elaborate trappings, stood at the open door, a wicked smile on his lips. With a wave of his baton the others rushed at Balzan.

An ordinary man would have been stunned by surprise and defeated easily, but not Balzan. His lightning reflexes went instantly into action. No time to unsnap his therb; before he had it out, they would be upon him. His only chance lay in instant attack.

A kick sent a bench whirling against two of the Krells as they rushed forward. They fell in a cursing tangle. Balzan dodged a sword stroke of one of the other four and smashed his fist into the man's face before he could recover his balance. Balzan felt the Krell's bones crack from the blow, which sent him crashing back onto his advancing comrades.

Taking advantage of the confusion, Balzan burst through the struggling men, reeled, and grabbed the table. With a muscle-wrenching heave, he hurled it into the faces of the stunned Krells.

Swords clattered to the floor, and cries of pain rent the air. Ledan had retreated outside the hut and stared in bewilderment at the savage creature he had encountered.

The lull in the combat gave Balzan time to unsheath his sword and snatch out his knife with his left hand. He did not wait for the Krells to renew their attack. Rushing in to attack, he caved in the ribs of one, still down on his hands and knees, with a savage kick.

As he parried a thrust with his knife, a savage swipe of his sword sheared off a Krell ear. The man crumpled to the floor screaming, gouts of blood spurting. The others advanced warily in a half circle. One feinted at Balzan's legs but was driven into the hut wall by a counter-blow that exposed his intestines. At that instant the three remaining Krells rushed.

Balzan ripped viciously upward and was rewarded by a hoarse gurgling scream. Two slashes followed and two more Krells were dead at Balzan's feet.

Behind him a shadow moved and as he instinctively leaped aside, a sword gashed his left arm. He clutched at his arm and saw it was the leader who had attempted to kill him from behind.

Balzan stepped out of the hut to close with his foe. The Orathians were massed outside. They offered no help; they were merely spectators.

The Krell confronting him rushed forward lifting his sword. As Balzan parried it, the man cleverly swung his caron, smashing into Balzan's face and sending him onto his back. The Krell shrieked in triumph and rushed again. Balzan's foot shot out and caught the attacker in his groin.

With cat-like speed Balzan sprang to his feet. The almond-skinned warrior rushed again, eyes blazing, lips foaming with impassioned hatred. He lunged savagely, but Balzan ripped into the Krell's torso with a quick and murderous thrust. The Krell's mouth flew open in pain, his sword fell to the ground. He looked at the youth before him in amazement. Then, his caron fell; a moment later he doubled up and followed it.

Blood flowed down the side of Balzan's face. His left arm was red with gore. An approaching Krell warrior who had been searching among the herds saw his commander sprawled at Balzan's feet. He whirled to flee. Balzan reversed his sword and hurled it like a javelin. The point smashed into the man's back. He pitched forward, the sword upright in his back and a stream of blood running from his mouth.

Balzan was surrounded now only by dead enemies. He relaxed. A voice behind him caused him to wheel in a flash. It was Taza, the Chronicler.

"And it was you who said that he had nothing to offer the Orathians," the old man smiled.

"I certainly didn't get any help from you," Balzan replied savagely. "There wasn't one man among you who fought beside me."

"But there are plenty who will, Balzan of Endore."

"Where?" Balzan rasped, wincing from the pain in his arm. "I see nothing but old men and cowards."

"In this village, yes," the Chronicler replied. "But I can take you to many that are only awaiting the signal and they will fight."

"Is this your governor?" Balzan motioned to the corpse at his feet.

"No, he wears the tunic of a Krell Counsel. That is probably his airship moored on the tower."

Balzan slumped wearily to a bench beside the hut. A thought struck him. Why not help these people? The Krells had attempted twice to kill him. Now they were his enemies also.

Tarlene appeared and handed him a cup of wine. He smiled at her and drained the cup. He set it down, wiped his mouth, and turned his blue eyes on the old man.

"All right, I will aid you. How long will it be before more Krells come from the tower?"

"We have most of the day. There are only three cohorts left. Two are on patrol and you just eliminated the third," the Chronicler chuckled.

"You mean the tower is undefended?" Balzan asked incredulously.

"Why not? No one would dare molest it. The governor's wife is the Krell ruler's daughter, and no one has weapons in this village."

Balzan tried to grasp the whole picture behind the incident. He did not intend to wait until the Krells returned.

"Then if it's war on the Krells, let's finish it. The governor will be next," said Balzan as he strode to the tower.

Balzan swept up the stairs, taking three at a stride. He knew that the quarters of the governor were situated at the top. As he reached there he broke the ornate door before him into splinters with one swift kick.

He found himself in the anteroom of the governor's quarters. Crossing the floor swiftly, he smashed through the chamber door and strode inside.

At a table in the middle of the glass-domed room stood a tall almond-skinned man of middle age. Balzan knew immediately that this was the Krell Governor. Silken divans stood about on the marble floor. On one table sat a flagon of wine with two filled goblets.

A woman rested on the divan. Her wide dark eyes held no trace of fear as she stared at the intruder.

With a curse, the governor unsheathed a jeweled dagger and advanced toward Balzan.

"You Orathian dog, you dare to enter my chambers?" He whipped the dagger forward in a swift arching stroke. Balzan just missed having his throat slit by the whistling edge. Parrying with a savage blow, he sent the Krell flying backward.

"A man should know who his executioner is, Krell. I am not an Orathian."

"Whoever you are, dog, you will soon be dead at my feet," Chalak sneered.

In the exchange of blows and thrusts, Chalak soon realized that he was up against a formidable opponent.

He was faced by a youth with lightning-quick speed and something Chalak had not seen on an Orathian face before —a look of fearlessness.

Chalak began to tire and, when he sensed the youth was only toying with him, his eyes filled with fear. With a sudden snarl he flung the blade at Balzan's face and darted for the far wall. There, his fingers probed for the switch that opened a hidden exit.

Balzan avoided the blade with a jerk of his head. He unsnapped his therb and it cracked. The poisoned barbs tore into the weak flesh of the governor. He screamed only once, then flopped to the floor.

Sweating and panting, Balzan turned to the woman on the divan.

Lenor had not moved during the struggle. Now she rose, eyes shining, raised her arms, and came fearlessly toward Balzan, ignoring the bloodsoaked tunic. She pressed herself against his young muscular body and twined her arms around his neck.

She was a beautiful creature, scented, adorned in golden silk. Balzan's blood ran swiftly through his veins at her touch.

"Who are you who fights like Androth himself, without fear? Are you a young god from Zetar?"

The dark eyes, under the long lashes, regarded him without fear. She drew away gently. Turning her back to him she emptied the contents of one of her jeweled rings into one of the wine goblets.

She handed it to Balzan and began sipping the other herself. She was a beautiful and intelligent woman and possessed a musical voice. "Will you not tell me your name, young god?"

Balzan stared into her eyes and sipped the wine. "I am Balzan of Endore and it was a man, not a god, that killed your husband."

Then Balzan hurled the goblet to the floor and furiously turned upon the woman. He had tasted the bitterness of the potion she had put into the wine. His hand fastened itself in her long black hair. Then he staggered as the drug took effect. She slipped from his reach as he fell heavily to the marble floor.

Lenor nodded in satisfaction. For the next few hours the young savage would be like a dead man. Swift action was now necessary.

She went to the window and peered below. Orathians were assembled in mass. Swiftly she collected her wits. She knew Ledan's airship crew was above at the mooring site. They were bound by orders never to leave the *Razon* unguarded. She would make good her escape by the ship. Within a short time after she reached the city, her father would lay siege to the Orathians. Secretly, she was glad to be rid of her vain, weak husband. Still, he was a Krell and must be avenged.

She grabbed a robe from one of her chests and donned it. Thrusting aside the corpse of her late husband, she searched with swift hands for the switch that activated the secret exit.

With a grating sound, a section of the wall swung inward, disclosing a spiral staircase leading upward.

The warriors guarding the airship came to attention as she appeared upon the roof.

"I journey at once upon the *Razon* for the city of Manator. Your commander is dead, as is my husband. Two of you, go to the chambers below. There you will find an Orathian I have drugged. Bind him and bring him aboard the ship. We will then depart for the city."

The captain saluted and ordered two men to fetch the prisoner. Lenor then climbed the rope ladder. The men prepared the ship for travel. The commander of the *Razon* loved his trim craft that was the pride of the Krell air fleet. He also had a precious cargo, Androth's daughter herself. He would see that she reached Manator alive and well.

The warriors appeared with the unconscious Balzan, carrying him beneath the armpits and legs. He was placed aboard and Lenor gave the command for the ship to depart.

The commander gave the order. "Cut away."

Word was passed across the deck and over the side to the Krell warriors below. Keen swords struck simultaneously, and instantly three strands of cable fell away below the gun turrets to the roof. The keen edges of the swords then severed the mooring line.

The *Razon,* her propellers whirling, lifted into the sky. She skimmed through the air like a gentle projectile. The buoyancy tanks above her stern kept the ship level and caused her occupants no airsickness.

Lenor smiled inwardly as she settled herself comfortably into a chair. In a few hours her prisoner would be in the darkest dungeon in Manator. Her dark eyes flashed triumphantly as she gazed on Balzan's prostrate form.

* * *

The forbidding walls of the Royal Palace of Manator rose in jagged silhouette against the darkening sky. Warriors strode along the battlements, swords on hips, vigilant, their eyes studying the city that the castle commanded.

In his private apartment, Androth, King of the Krells, sat in solitary meditation. His jutting forehead was lined from the thoughts that were dark and heavy upon his soul. He opened his yellow eyes and expelled his breath; he opened and closed his hands several times and prepared for his ritual.

The massive room was lit only by a single flickering candle. He began mouthing incantations. Androth sat straight-backed in an ornate jeweled chair; the muscles of his face stood out with the tensions of his deep inner-directed concentration. After many moments, a picture began to take shape somewhere behind his eyes.

It blurred and shimmered, then began to focus. It was an airship—the *Razon*—cutting through a clear moonlit sky. With a greater effort, Androth brought the ship nearer in his mind.

Closer and closer until he saw the emblem of his own image upon it. With the vision firmly locked in his mind, Androth saw his daughter Lenor and, bound at her feet, the unconscious form of an Orathian. Only Androth knew that the man was not an Orathian, but something alien, strong, and a threat to his power.

Androth's strained face broke the vision and he shook his head. Sweat dropped onto the table. He was bathed in perspiration. His effort was prodigious and he ached. Then he shuddered and, completely spent and exhausted, slumped forward on the table. Then he tapped lightly upon a bronze disc with a wooden stick.

Presently the summons was answered by a servant who reverently entered his king's chambers.

Seeing his sovereign motionless over a table, he edged nervously toward him. "My King," he said, and gently touched Androth's shoulder. Androth leaned back in the chair. The sight of Androth's face shocked him, for it had aged. There was no doubt in the servant's mind that his king looked several years older now than he had earlier this evening. Heavy wrinkles lined his mouth and brow, and his hair had lightened about the temples. The servant was not overly alarmed since it was a usual occurrence to him.

Whenever the Feast of Zetar approached, the king always changed his appearance, but when he returned from his retreat in the sacred mountain, his youth and vigor were always at their peak. His servant was one of the privileged few who ever gazed upon Androth in this condition. His silence was never broken, as the king would have him executed for any breach of trust.

Androth's eyes suddenly opened. "What—?"

"You summoned me, my King. It is I, Leoh," the servant said softly.

Androth pushed his chair back and rose slowly. His yellow eyes looked haunted. "The *Razon* will be mooring shortly. My daughter is aboard. When she arrives in the palace, tell her I am aware of the events that have brought

40

her home. I will give her audience in the morning. Now, I must rest."

Androth collapsed upon his bed. He would deal with the alien. After all, he reminded himself, the rewards were always far greater than the sacrifices required of him. He ruled an empire. One alien would never disrupt it. Soon he was in a deep sleep, void of visions or troubles. As he slept his features slowly continued to age.

* * *

At the edge of the city a young League Captain placed his finger to his tongue and tasted the water that was flowing from one of the city's many outlets. He made a wry mouth and turned to the warrior beside him.

"Yes, that is rust, and the water is too warm. Someone is forging weapons. This must be reported immediately to Counsel Emor."

* * *

Below the city in the catacombs that honeycombed the metropolis, weapons were being forged by assembled Orathians and Corillians. The swords were crude, but adequate. The men were to put their deadly arms to work soon. Standing beside a huge Corillian, pounding a sword that was white hot, a tall young Orathian known as Jem studied the charts of the city.

Jem's village was a herdsmen compound for the Krells. He was content in knowing that his mother and sister were safe. The herdsmen were seldom used as mine slaves except as punishment and women were never used.

Jem had dark brown hair and gray-blue eyes. He was muscular and was a dedicated revolutionary. He was determined to free his people from the shackles of their Krell masters.

His study of the charts was disturbed by the appearance of one of his comrades. Arc, an Orathian from a neighboring village, had grown up with him and, like him, was also an exile from his tribe. Both men were close to the same age, yet they had completely different ideas about freedom.

Jem believed that only violence could free his people. Arc advocated passive resistance and negotiations with th

41

Krells. He looked at Jem and then at the weapon being hammered into shape.

"Still forging metals, I see."

"Of course," Jem answered.

"But while the metal cools . . . think Jem. You have heard Taza, your Chronicler, you have heard him speak."

"Speak?" Jem rasped. "He speaks only of peace. He wishes to lull the Krells to their death with boredom."

"The days of the Feast of Zetar approach. Androth goes to retreat. At this time it is allowed for all slaves to receive counsel from their tribal Chroniclers."

"So?" Jem answered sullenly. "The Chroniclers are puppets that kneel down like vermin to Androth. Piety is their teaching. I am fire, they are water, how can we ever agree?"

Arc spread his hands in a gesture of hopelessness. "The days that Androth is in the bowels of the mountain such crowds will gather as never before. The Chroniclers will appear before the assembled people and present our case. Then stand with them. Let your strength be known, but keep your swords sheathed. Then when the Chronicler's message of unity and peace sweeps through the city, Androth will listen to our case. How can he refuse?"

Jem stared at his friend. He wished with all his heart that he felt the same, but he did not. Yet, he did not want his plans altered.

"If the Chroniclers can perform that magic and save the spilling of blood for our people, I agree."

Arc smiled, then, with a look of suspicion, touched his friend's arm.

"You will give them time?"

"Yes."

"You will let them at least . . . speak?"

"Yes."

Arc cast his eyes upward and then smiled with all his heart at Jem. "That will be a day to be remembered."

He then disappeared into the shadows, content with the knowledge that he had averted useless carnage.

When he was certain that his friend had departed, Jem smiled wickedly.

"It will be remembered."

The other workman turned to him with a look of bewilderment upon his face. "What do you mean, Jem?"

Jem waved him to silence. "Quiet Arc is a dreamer, and all dreamers are fools. This is the hour we have been waiting for. The Chroniclers bring us our audience, we'll borrow them."

He then opened his scroll of charts. "We'll run them through the city this way and that way. Your people, Sefa," he said, pointing to a comrade beside him, "you'll take the east wall; Mika, you the west. I, myself, will stay at the edge of the city. We will kill many Krells. Quickly, done and over with. We will give the crowd back to the Chroniclers."

Jem then picked up a sword and balanced it in his hand. His eyes swept the men before him who were looking at each other as if for comfort in numbers. Jem smiled to all of them and held the sword outstretched. "Now, isn't that fair?"

Chapter Five

His head spinning, stomach racked with nausea, and throat on fire, Balzan slowly regained his senses. He only had a vague memory of the tower and of the beautiful Krell woman. Now he found himself gazing at wet black walls, listening to the squeak of scampering rats, as he sat up on a bed of moldy straw. As he moved, there was a jingle of chains linking his wrists and ankles to a massive stone slab set in the wall.

His head ached intensely. His mouth was dry, his tongue stuck to his palate from thirst, and pangs of hunger assailed him. Reacting against his imprisonment with rage, he savagely tossed his chains against the wall.

There was the sound of footsteps and the jingling of keys. His jailer, a huge hulk of a man, appeared on the other side of the iron grille that barred the door of the cell.

"Where am I?" Balzan demanded.

The jailer sneered. "Where you soon will wish you weren't, Orathian dog. You are in the dungeons of King Androth's palace at Manator. Here, eat. It may be the last you get."

Thrusting a loaf and a small jug through the bars, the Krell went away, his laughter resounding hollowly in the corridor.

Balzan slumped back on the bed and bit into the stale loaf. He washed it down with gulps of water. The sounds of pain and dying were on all sides of him. He was in the prison of the damned. The Abyss. Where insects darted and scrabbled, where the rats gnawed dead men's bones, where the vermin clustered in dark corners awaiting fresh meat.

He pondered his predicament. Now, through a woman's treachery and cleverness, he was at the mercy of the Krells.

He was chained like an animal, but he had many companions in misery. The corridor was lined with cells. Below him the dungeons descended to twelve more sub-levels and the damned lived in every one. Until their lives mercifully ended, chains rattled and clanked dismally. The prisoners were starving. They were like the walking dead—hairy, filthy, and covered with sores. Men were moaning, some screaming, as chains rattled on the stones.

Balzan's eyes narrowed as the clank of footsteps sounded in the corridor. At a sharp command the steps halted. Through the grille Balzan saw Krell warriors in the torchlight, swords in their hands. Two held weapons that Balzan had never seen before. They resembled what the teacher had described as weapons that fired steel projectiles by an igniting of black powder. They, like the caron, were also silver. A tall massive officer stepped forward, a coil of whip hanging loosely in his hand. He spoke in a sharp cutting voice. "Unshackle the Orathian and be wary of him."

Two warriors stepped into his cell. They unshackled him from the wall and then rechained his wrists in front. Balzan twitched with eagerness to attack the men, but held himself in check. The warrior captain hissed, "One move, Orathian, and you are dead."

Balzan's blue eyes regarded the Krell without emotion as the warriors pushed him into the corridor. "I want you to know one thing, Krell. I am not an Orathian. You can cease attempting to frighten me. You only make me laugh."

The Krell's face twitched in fury as he spat back, "You dare open that filthy mouth to a Krell as an equal. I'll teach you a lesson in manners you'll never forget."

He whipped his caron from his belt and with his lips pulled back in a canine fashion, he laughed a shrill uncontrolled laugh. He touched the cool metal to Balzan's face. When the youth merely smiled back at him in disgust, the Krell went berserk.

He brought the whip handle up and rammed it savagely into Balzan's stomach. Balzan doubled over in agony. Then a blow smashed against the back of his head and he fell forward. He spun clumsily. He saw the look of pure ecstasy in the Krell's eyes. Balzan's hatred exploded as he reached up against the dead weight of iron and grabbed the whip from the stunned officer, then brought the handle down across his face.

The Krell toppled back, spouting blood, shrieking. Balzan then leaped into the center of the corridor and raced for the guardroom. He stopped and uncoiled the whip. He lashed out at the pursuing guards. One was caught around the neck and Balzan dragged him forward, breaking his neck. The jailer appeared behind Balzan and coiled his lash across the floor and tripped the youth. Balzan bent, grabbed the whip, and pulled; before the jailer could let go Balzan smashed his knee into the huge Krell's groin. Then he brought his manacled fists down on the jailer's neck. His head hung strangely before he pitched to the floor. Then the entire cohort leaped on Balzan.

The whip was smashed from his grip, hands grabbed him and twisted him over. The Krell captain raised his baton and smashed it viciously into Balzan's face. He was once again in blackness.

* * *

He was revived by stagnant water splashing from a bucket into his face. The Krell loomed over him. Balzan snickered as he saw that the officer's face was covered with blood.

At a gesture to the warriors, Balzan was lifted up and marched along the dank corridor. Balzan knew it would be futile to struggle so he moved along without resistance, but his mind was concentrating on what to do next.

Winding stone staircases led upward. Up he was dragged, throttled in the chains. At each level stood an armed guard cradling the caron in his arms.

Balzan got a glimpse of the outside world as they passed window slits. The palace was built on a crag overlooking the sea. He heard the surf pounding the rocks below. The dungeons were carved out of the rock whose face ended in the lapping waves below.

Then they were in the palace itself. They passed endless rooms, each a marvel in its own. Now their steps echoed on marble floors. There were fountains and flowers that exuded heavy perfumes. Warriors stood every few paces, their weight balanced on golden lances they held at attention. They paused for a moment before two immense doors, then with the sound of a bronze plate being struck, the doors slowly opened.

46

Balzan was pulled onto a wide and shining floor. Sunlight glanced down, emerald and scarlet. There was a great assembly of people. All eyes were on Balzan. Balzan eyed them back, afire with curiosity. The men were bedecked in jeweled and gilded leather tunics. All was a dazzlement to the youth. He could barely stand. He was weak. He tottered and fell; the Krell officer kicked him up. Balzan tried to rise, but fell again. The officer motioned to the two guards who then started dragging him. He left a bloody trail across the shining floor.

Balzan looked up. He saw a throne, distorted, on its side, soaring above him. It appeared to reach the ceiling of the immense room. The throne was ablaze with brilliance, it shattered the light into a myriad of brightnesses. A figure sat on the throne, a blaze of gold and silver. A second throne stood at the side, smaller, but just as splendid.

The youth was aware of the hum of conversation and stray words sprouted up, like Orathian dog, assassin, Chalak's killer. The warriors moved back. A wedge of emerald green gave a backdrop to the thrones. Balzan saw the blurs of many almond faces. Jewels glittered into his eyes like fire and ice.

The Krell officer's voice boomed close.

"Here, Great Monitor, is the Orathian assassin that our beloved Princess Lenor has delivered for your justice."

Balzan tried to stand erect, he wished to show the Krells nothing but his defiance, contempt; he tried, but the chains were dragging him down. He staggered and fell. He was lifted up again and he fought to stay erect.

The Monitor was a huge man with a thin cruel mouth. His forehead jutted to the extreme and his stern and gloomy features gave Balzan the impression that the man was of a mystical origin.

At his right, on the smaller throne, sat a woman. Balzan felt his blood run hot with recognition. Lenor! Her voluptuous body was draped in a seductive gown that befit the princess of such a magnificent palace. A diamond of fantastic proportion adorned her lustrous black hair.

Balzan's eyes were aflame as he stared at her. Every inch of his body expressed the contempt he felt.

Lenor's eyes fastened triumphantly on the trussed and helpless figure of her captive. The Monitor spoke with the raspy sound of age, yet he appeared in a strange way ageless.

"This Orathian smells worse than the Staykton. Tell me, Orathian, are the beasts your parents?"

Lenor joined in the laughter of the court at the jest uttered by the Monitor.

Balzan stood still and upright, his eyes narrowed to a slit as he watched the Monitor turn to Lenor. "My Princess, could you have been in error? This creature hardly appears to be able to combat a herdsman's daughter, let alone slay your mighty Chalak."

Lenor tossed a glance to Balzan. "He is cunning and possesses great strength. I wish his death to be particularly painful."

The Monitor bowed. "The daughter of our Supreme Master is not only beautiful, but possesses a warrior's heart as well."

Balzan's voice boomed at the Monitor. "If I am to die by the hands of scum, I wish to die with it known that I am not one of your sniveling race of cowards that call themselves Orathians."

"That is very enlightening," the Monitor replied in a mocking tone. "Who, then, do we hold captive that smells of Staykton and has the appearance of a chalk animal?"

"I am Balzan of Endore. I am alien to this world. To explain it would be beyond the likes of you, a race that is gluttonous with power and forced servitude."

"You speak with words of bravery, a uniqueness in Orathians, yet you are plainly mad."

"Mad?" Balzan repeated. "I offered the Krells my friendship and was attacked. If I had any small part in destroying your web of slavery, then I die in joy."

"Oh, you will die, my young friend, but not in joy. You are an enigma to me, Balzan of Endore."

"In what way?"

"There's a strange inconsistency in a man who offers friendship and then kills my governor."

"I believe that no man has the right to enslave another and that in time your empire will fall around your neck like the chains you have placed on your slaves."

"Eloquent, but impractical. What race would dare challenge the empire of Androth?"

"Androth?" Balzan sneered. "It appears you are the ruler

here, since I see no king, only his daughter, whom I should have slain with her cowardly husband."

Black rage seethed in the Monitor's face as he saw the disdain in the face of the youth before him.

"Hold your tongue, dog, or I shall cut it from your insolent mouth this instant."

"Then come and do so, old man, if you can hobble down from your chair," Balzan roared as he flexed his taut muscles.

The Monitor rose and started to descend the steps. He was stopped by the blare of trumpets across the huge hall. The Monitor turned as an avenue opened through the milling mass and a warrior, bowing to the Monitor, handed him a golden scroll. A frown creased his huge jutting forehead. He looked down at Balzan fleetingly, then handed the parchment to Lenor.

"The fates smile upon you, Balzan of Endore. Our Supreme Master Androth has ordered you to be confined until he returns from his retreat. You will have the opportunity to continue your hatred of us for a while longer. Take the dog from my sight."

Balzan saw Lenor stalk angrily from the hall and smiled inwardly. For the present, anyway, he would remain alive. Why, the troubled youth wondered.

Why would the king of the Krells decide to let him live, unless he had grislier plans in mind for him.

"I will see you before me again, Orathian. And when that time comes you will curse your mother for having given birth to you."

The grim words from the Monitor followed Balzan as he left the throne room.

Out of the room hurried the knot of guards. Balzan was surrounded by a wall of men. He was aware of the infernal aches in his body as well as his seething hatred.

When they reached the dark entrance to the dungeons, the escort turned Balzan over to the jailer and two assistants standing in the dark.

As they grasped him and led him under the grained ceilings, along corridors and down again into the bowels of the palace, Balzan's spirits fell to their lowest ebb.

When they reached a small antechamber with an octagon of light casting down upon them, the man beside Balzan coughed.

They dropped him. He fell to the floor and rolled. His head rang, but he got to his hands and tried to stand up.

The jailer shrieked, "What are you doing?"

Balzan focused his eyes to see that the jailer and one guard were dead. He saw the hooded man with a bloody sword in his hand. He advanced toward Balzan. He removed his hood and Balzan saw that it was not an almond-skinned Krell, but an Orathian, an Orathian who had just dispatched two Krells as silently as a cat and as deadly.

Balzan's brain reeled.

"Who are you?" he gasped.

"Does it matter, Balzan of Endore, who I am as long as I enjoy killing Krells?"

Balzan shook his head. His hands trembled. He could see them before him, shaking against the stone where a trickle of blood flowed from a corpse.

"Well, do you want to stay here with your Krell friends or do you prefer to breathe a little clean air?"

All Balzan could muster, in his weakened condition, was a weak nod.

The Orathian lifted Balzan up, hoisted him to his chest, and carried him through the corridors that led from the palace of Manator.

After a while, he brought Balzan to a small space where he laid him on a bed of straw; there he brought water, bathed him, and ministered to his wounds. Balzan saw an anvil and hammer in the foreground.

"I will be able to get some rest now that I have saved Tarlene's god," he said as he looked into Balzan's face and smiled. Then he snapped the manacles that held Balzan with one mighty swing of a hammer. He lifted the iron anvil to the side and tossed the hammer. "Surprised?"

"Tarlene—" Balzan reached a hand up and grasped the stranger's forearm.

The stranger smiled and continued bathing the wounds. "She was afraid that she had lost the love of her life." Then a look of furtiveness crossed his face, "And she almost did."

"Who are you?" Balzan asked.

"I am Jem of Rashton."

"You are Tarlene's brother?"

He nodded and continued with the swab. "Taza holds you in great esteem, my friend. I do also. You saved my sister's life and avenged my mother's death. For as long as I hold life in my body I will be your friend and fight at your side."

"How did you hear of me?"

"Taza sent a courier from the Corillians. I have been in the city these past days assembling followers to crush Androth and his dogs."

"But . . ."

Jem smiled and tilted a cup to Balzan's lips. It held cold water that tasted to the parched youth like fine Uran wine.

"When word of your exploits reached our village, I entered the dungeons by the sea wall. The fortress was built to keep prisoners from getting out. It is easy to get in."

Balzan looked at him.

"I thank you, Jem, for saving me. I am ashamed that I thought all of your people to be cowards."

"My people have been held in the Krell servitude for many years. There had always been revolts, but since the last Krell feast my people have become docile. It is the magic that Androth receives from the mountain. Take the caron; it is worthless metal, yet it terrifies my people."

"Yes, I know. I discovered that from your sister," Balzan said.

"That mountain holds the answer, Balzan. It has to be destroyed. I have a skirmish planned on the day our Chroniclers arrive in the city."

"But you have no weapons."

"We're making them. We also have men working on a machine that can knock Androth's airships out of the sky."

"Taza mentioned it to me," Balzan replied, "but he lacks confidence in it being restored."

Jem threw back his head and laughed. "That old man is suspicious of anything that he does not understand. It is true we have had difficulty. Perhaps you could help us if you wish. If you do not, I understand and hold no grudge against you. You already have served the Orathians as a warrior and friend. We expect nothing more from you."

Balzan studied the face of the man before him. It had strength and character in it. He extended his hand in friendship. "If I can help you free your people from slavery, I will do so with all my heart."

The Orathian firmly grasped Balzan's outstretched hand. "As soon as you have rested and your strength has returned, I will take you to the complex where the machine lays. Now we must get to a place of safety. The Krells will be searching these corridors at any moment."

In the dead of night, with the two moons hanging low in the sky, Balzan was conveyed out of the palace and led to the catacombs where Jem's small army of Orathians and Corillians awaited. Balzan now felt that once again he was in the company of men—men who would fight and, if need be, die to end their oppression.

* * *

The king of the Krells shivered in his chambers. The room seemed to tremble under his feet. He knew that if he wished to accomplish his goal he must hasten. Speaking to his daughter Lenor through a black transparent drapery to spare her the shock of seeing his condition, he rose and rubbed his arms; he was cold.

It had been a comfort talking to her, but he must not linger since her news that the alien had escaped tore at his mind.

"We will find him, daughter, and your revenge will be sweet, I promise you."

Lenor gestured to speak, but Androth raised his hand to silence her. "Later, daughter. Now I must rest. We will talk again tomorrow."

His words were a dismissal and Lenor stalked from his chambers.

Androth moved to the terrace of his chambers and let the night wind fan his face. He was cold, yet he was perspiring. His strength was fading with each hour. He grasped the iron rungs in front of him until his knuckles turned white. He knew that his only salvation lay in the mountain, but he was reluctant to enter until the feast began. With his rapid deterioration, he feared he must break the tradition and journey immediately to his sanctuary.

The wind grew cold suddenly and he shuddered from the recurrent blasts. He peered down at the dark land and thought grimly that there would be a time when he would not be able to reverse the aging process and he would wither and die like any other Krell. The thought put him into the grip of depression. The wind lessened, but only slightly, and his nausea-racked body seemed to be fading into the darkness itself. He resolved to leave for the mountain at once. Then he remembered the escaped alien and the fear returned like a cold embrace. First he would call upon his powers to search out the alien, who would be imprisoned until he could have time to analyze him from inside the mountain's vast resources. The cold gripped him again and he grew faint and staggered. He felt as if he were falling, plunging into the blackness of his own tormented soul.

He struggled against it and called his servant's name.

Chapter Six

The flagship *Zetar* touched the outer end of the docking platform; slaves rushed onto the dock and gathered in the mooring cables and attached them to the metal pillars lining the platform. A cohort of warriors lowered the ladder and hurried down to take their positions. A moment later Master Counsel Emor appeared; the warriors snapped to attention as he descended. His aide, Commander Muros, stood awaiting his warrior chief.

"Greetings, great Emor," Muros inclined his head. "We bless your glorious return to the city. The Monitor awaits you in his chambers."

"Let him," Emor laughed. "First I am going to bathe and dine."

Counsel Emor was a tall man, a muscular and awesome figure. He was dressed in a golden tunic with the red circle of Androth signifying his impressive rank as First Warrior of Manator, the Protector of the Empire. He was a man of ambition, great wealth, and power. The Monitor was his only rival for Androth's favor. While the Monitor sat in splendor, Emor added to Androth's vast empire by sacking and murdering, thereby adding immensely to the wealth of the Krells.

Muros fell into step beside Emor as he crossed the mooring dock toward the palace roof. As they walked, Emor removed his helmet and ran his hand through his hair. It was evident the great soldier was fatigued. "The trek was particularly nasty this time, Muros. I had to completely level the reptilian city. I lost four ships, and who knows how many more will fail to return. I want an hourly report on all the fleet that arrives today."

"The Monitor will be pleased, Counsel."

Emor glared at him. "That fool? How he continually sways the Forum and stays in favor with Androth is beyond me."

"He has a powerful voice, Lord Emor. Do not discount him as a fool."

"And you, Muros? How have you fared as my representative in the Forum during my absence?"

"Splendidly. I have news that will please you and add glory to your name."

"Tell me later, first I want to shed this tunic. My body offends me, it has been days since I have bathed."

Muros was about to remind him of the Monitor, but then he thought better of it and asked instead, "Were the reptilian cities as barbaric as claimed?"

Emor laughed. "Every city is barbaric compared to Manator, my young comrade. Tell me, has the Master entered retreat as yet?"

"We have not been informed that he has, Lord Emor. However, the time draws near."

Emor shared his bath and steam with Muros. Emor had always found Muros pleasant and affable, and he had that winning manner which seeks for the opinions of others, even when the others are persons of no particular interest. Muros sat aloft, reclining in the steam vapors and sweating profusely, but completely content. Emor lolled in the bath, treading water lazily, floating back and forth, luxuriating in the warm scented water. Emor's body was well kept—not paunchy, but flat and hard—and he was youthful and alert. Relaxed now, he asked of his aide what news he had for him.

"The Orathians are revolting and Chalak was assassinated. They had the culprit in irons, but he escaped."

Emor smiled. "Chalak's passing will cause no mourning. Lenor, our beloved princess, must be delighted."

"She eagerly awaits your return, my lord. It appears this particular Orathian is of vital concern to her."

"In what way?"

"She hates him with a venom I shudder at. She escaped with her life by drugging him. She also has offered a quadrant for his capture."

"A full quadrant?" Emor smiled. "He must have angered her. Beneath that beautiful face lies a person to be reckoned with."

"Also, my lord, it has been discovered that the rabble are forging weapons in the catacombs."

"They are no threat. We have dealt with them before and we shall again. Now I am famished, let us dine."

* * *

He climbed out of the bath, and the Orathian slave women waiting there enveloped him in warm towels. Emor gazed at the women; his attitude toward them was as pets. His people had divested them of most elements of equality. It was a subtle conditioning, but Androth had succeeded beyond measure.

They were dressed in short plain tunics that were damp from the steam of the bath, and spotted with perspiration from their efforts. Emor drew one of them to him and fondled her breasts. He smiled down at her, while she cringed against him but made no resistance.

He then walked to the rubbing table and lay down. A moment later Muros joined him.

"I am delighted that an Orathian has Princess Lenor angry," Emor said.

"Well, she will soon have her revenge, Lord Emor, and you will be richer."

Emor stretched and luxuriated under the clever kneading fingers of the masseuse. One woman held a pitcher of scented oil, pouring a constant, careful lubrication under the fingers of the masseuse, who flexed the tension out of muscle after muscle. Emor twisted like a great cat being stroked, sighing with pleasure. He looked lazily up at Muros.

"How will this Orathian's capture make me richer, Muros?"

The warrior beamed. "Because of my loyalty and dedication to you, Lord Emor."

The Counsel smiled reflectively. "Yes, I am aware of that. But you speak in riddles."

"Congratulate me. Better yet, you can congratulate both of us."

"Really?"

"Tomorrow I lead an assault upon the Orathians."

Emor looked up at his aide. The muscles on his neck bulged with passion, and passion was all over his body as he exploded. "Great hosts of Zetar, you are going to do *what?*"

Muros, stunned by his lord's wrath, smiled with confusion as he answered.

"I'm leaving to punish the Orathians that assassinated Chalak. The entire city is going to bless our trek."

Emor was off the table in an instant. With a savage gesture he dismissed the servants. His rage seething, he then turned to the trembling and thoroughly confused Muros.

"And whose brilliant idea was this?" he rasped.

"Why . . . the Monitor."

"Hah! I should have known. And tell me this, who is to be in command of the garrison at Manator while you are slave-hunting?"

"A counsel from the Monitor's personal guard."

"Brilliant. He not only totally immobilizes me in the Forum, but ties my hands at the garrison as well. I underestimated the old man—and overestimated you, Muros," he said with an ugly scowl on his face.

Muros, in shock and offering placation, rasped out, "Your fleet is at the base of the city."

Emor looked at him in amazement. "My fleet? Do you think I would enter Manator during the Feast, at the head of my warriors?"

"Well, Jazor did."

"Jazor?" the Counsel roared. "To the infamy of his name, to the utter damnation of his soul. Androth would have my head on a skewer for such a desecration."

"Then I will refuse to go."

Emor shook his head in disgust.

"No. One of the disadvantages of being an officer in my service is his word. You pledged the Forum to go and go you must, but the city tribute is impossible. Let's not add the trappings of a fool to our predicament. Leave tonight. Assemble your men. Go to the ships by unfrequented streets. Go without any fanfare. Not even a drum." He paused and drew his breath . . . "Sneak out."

Through with his bath, shaved, perfumed, his hair oiled slightly and curled delicately, his tunic silk and gold and fresh for dinner, Emor went to his solarium to have a glass of wine before dinner. The room was rose colored with a delicately tinted sun roof. The result at this time of day was a gentle glow of fading sunlight, which transformed the room into a fantasy of color. He sipped on his wine, still angered at his protégé's ignorance. Then he heard a familiar voice come from behind.

"Welcome back, Emor," she smiled in a combination of wickedness and real pleasure.

As he turned and saw her in her white gown, her dark hair coiffeured on top of her head, her almond skin gleaming in the fading light, a smile came to the Counsel's hard face.

"I was beginning to wonder if you were coming or not," he said in mock indifference.

She approached him with a feline gracefulness and put her soft arms around his neck. He drew her close and kissed her long and passionately. She smiled up at him and then took his wine goblet and finished its contents.

"My fahher has entered retreat, Emor, and I cannot tell you how relieved I am that you are back."

Emor smiled and put his hand upon her waist. "For yourself or for the well-being of Manator?"

"Both," Lenor answered. "My father is weak. He may never return from that mountain. If this happens, I want you here, and upon the notification of his death, I want the Monitor to be the next to die."

Emor sighed. "Is that all you want?"

Lenor answered him in a very pleasant manner.

* * *

Androth stood before the great mountain, the temple of the Krell god Zetar. Topped by four great carved faces, its entrance was awesome. Androth spread his arms and chanted: "The Feast of Zetar has begun and I, your servant, reappear for the enlightenment and wisdom of your most divine powers."

At the sound of his voice a flock of exotic birds whirled from among the carvings and screeched in the misty air above. They settled again in the tall trees and, as their cries died away, Androth became aware of a low moaning sound, like the agony of a thousand lost souls. It was the guardian of the Mountain Crixma.

Androth smiled and was not afraid. He and he alone knew the passage that led to safety. All others led to the jaws of the Crixma. The Crixma was the thing that nightmares were made of. A huge, six-legged anthropoid with saber-toothed fangs. Nothing could withstand the beast. For centuries he had guarded the mountain and guarded it well. For, except for Androth, no living creature had ever entered the temple and lived to tell of it.

Androth entered the temple and the darkness. The stone faces, impassive to the elements and time, were his only audience as he disappeared into the bowels of the mountain.

*　*　*

Three days later Balzan followed Jem across the countryside to the site of the dismantled machine they hoped to restore. They followed the river southward into the province of Corillia. Through the low rolling hills they traveled past canals and tree-hung banks where mirrored reflections gave strange duplicating effects as if the two men were walking on air.

Occasionally the water changed color as minerals washed down from the hills where the slave miners toiled for their Krell masters. Mostly the river reflected the sky and the clouds, the wild flowers, trees, and rushes of the banks. When they paused to drink, it was refreshing and tasted pure, clean, sweet. They left the river and entered the Corillian forest at midday. The country changed drastically. They were in a forest of tangled growths and vast sweeps of moorland. Carnivores also dwelt in these forests and Balzan and Jem kept their senses alert and their eyes sharp.

Balzan thought of his therb and Kharnite sword confiscated and held at the Krell palace. What he held now was little more than a bar of iron. It was shaped like a sword, but Balzan knew it would be inferior in close combat. Balzan cast a glance at his companion who was looking intently at the dense vegetation ahead.

"What is it?" Balzan asked.

Jem did not answer but continued probing the underbrush. His hand went to his scabbard and he unsheathed his sword. Balzan did likewise.

"That smell! I think we have a carnivore waiting in ambush," Jem exclaimed.

"I smell nothing."

"You have not lived your life in this forest as I have, Balzan, nor hunted the raxpore as I. I can smell it."

Then they saw it. It was huge and, upon sighting it, Balzan too smelled the repulsive odors of which it reeked. Jem did not hesitate but hurled himself at the beast, his sword held high and cocked over his shoulder.

The raxpore was a reptile. It was not a zanth, the reptiles that Balzan had stalked in Endoria. This one had a dozen or so bent and crooked legs; as it walked its body slung between them. Its scales were rimmed with a silvery iridescence. Its three eyes blinked rapidly. Jem slashed down at it. Balzan raced to its other side and struck at its head. Its tendrils groped forward, writhing, seeking to snatch and grip its prey into the convulsively chewing jaws that extended parallel to the rear of its ugly head. Balzan knew now what Jem meant by the smell. It was as horrible as the beast itself and Balzan would never forget it. It reeked with its own effluvia and the rotting stenches of its victims.

Jem struck again and again and then had to leap back as a tendril writhed out toward him. His blows had no apparent effect on the reptile. Balzan darted in, thrusting, trying to plunge into the top of the head. Thick ooze pulsed forth and Balzan retreated, gagging with the smell of vomit.

The reptile lashed its tail with tremendous force from side to side, splitting and pulverizing the small trees. Balzan thrust again and caught the right eye. It burst with a flow of a green slimy substance that showered Balzan as he dodged back.

A tendril engulfed Jem and drew him into the beast. Balzan sliced down with all his strength and severed it. The reptile shrieked hideously, but Jem was out of its grasp.

The shrieks and hissings screeched higher. Now both men began a systematic slashing away of the groping tentacles. The massive tail arched over Balzan and smashed into the ground an instant after Balzan leaped aside.

Jem sruck his sword into it, but it was futile. Balzan slashed and hacked and then blotted out the left eye. Now the reptile jerked back to protect its last remaining eye. Balzan kept thrusting and missing.

Jem moved in too close and the beast snared him with its forelegs. Its talons ripped into his tunic and Jem felt a white-hot pain in his side. Balzan moved in to the side of the trapped Orathian, whose body was now covered with the ooze. Balzan leaped and struck. A foreleg darted for him and only the reflex of the youth saved him as the foreleg gave him a glancing blow. It was enough to send him sprawling backward at least ten yards.

Balzan then leaped on his feet and charged again. He feinted to his left and then struck at the beast's right. The blade ripped into the foreleg, sending great spouts of ooze in the air. It released Jem and his unconscious body slumped to the ground.

Balzan then aimed for the remaining eye. The head twisted, reared, the fanged mouth hissed. Balzan sliced at the reptile's head as it stepped back again, protecting its last eye. That pause gave Balzan time to drag Jem out of the line of combat.

Now, in blind anger, the youth launched himself at the beast. He thrust at the eye again and again. All the thrusts were parried or blocked. Then he brought the sword down, cutting into the scales. The sword had little effect on the armored scales. The bulk inched ponderously forward. The fangs opened and closed, chewing angrily.

The reptile was no angrier than Balzan, however.

He leaped again, tried for the eye, missed, slashed down savagely; the sword pinged and broke. He threw the hilt at the eye but it bounced off the snout.

Behind the reptile's forelegs lay Jem's discarded sword. Balzan seized it, took a breath, and plunged again. This time the sword penetrated the center eye. It burst in a shower of ooze. Balzan slipped, then rolled away as a flailing claw reached for him. The reptile's screams shattered the forest in its blind rage. Balzan, in the grip of his own fury, plunged the sword deep into the reptile's only soft layer of skin—the throat. He leaned on it and thrust as hard as his muscles could push. The beast reared. Balzan, still clinging to the sword, reared with it. Then, his fingers slipped from the greasy hilt and he toppled back.

He clawed to his feet as the beast reared in its death agony. Then, with a final scream, it crashed down, gushing blood everywhere. Balzan staggered back, bruised, cut, and exhausted.

He limped over to Jem's body and saw that the wound had not penetrated any vital organs. He looked around in exhaustion. The forest was strange to him and, with a man of Jem's size, it would be impossible to attempt to carry him, and it would be unthinkable to leave him in his condition. Then he heard movement coming from the brush. He staggered to his feet and faced the direction of the sound. If it was another raxpore Balzan was ready to fight with his bare hands, if necessary.

The first thing he saw was the black robe and white beard so different from the green vegetation the form appeared from. It was Taza, the Chronicler, and behind him were several Corillians. Their appearance was a wonderful sight.

* * *

They reached the Corillian outpost shortly before dusk. Balzan saw Tarlene in the group of milling villagers. Upon seeing him she raced toward him. He gathered her in his arms. She smelled clean and sweet. He felt her warm soft arms embrace him even though he was covered with filth from the beast he had conquered.

"Oh Balzan . . . Balzan, you have come back to me." She held him close and began sobbing in joy. She kept saying his name and clasping him to her. Then she saw her brother's form on the makeshift stretcher.

"Jem."

She fell on her knees beside him, the tears streaming.

Taza put a wrinkled hand upon her shoulder. "He will be all right," he said soothingly. "Now quickly, get water and linen for his wounds."

Tarlene shook her head and then ran into the hut. Taza motioned the men to carry the stretcher after her. Then, putting his arm around Balzan, he led him into an adjoining hut.

"Rest, there is wine. I will attend to Jem and return presently."

Balzan drank directly from the jug. His throat was raw and parched. He could not remember when he had felt so exhausted. Replacing the jug on the small table, he collapsed onto the bed of straw behind him and was asleep instantly.

Chapter Seven

Balzan stirred after several hours of dreamless sleep. He got up from the bed and moved through the gloom of the hut. His head throbbed with the last vestiges of the pain he had suffered during the past days.

Outside the hut, in the pale light of dawn, he splashed water from the well over his face and shoulders, then drank deeply. Straightening, he paused. The village was quiet. Several camp fires still glowed. Balzan sat before one and fed wood to it until a cheerful and warming fire rose. He looked up and saw Taza emerging from a hut. Upon seeing the youth, he walked over and sat beside him.

The old man rubbed his wrinkled hands over the fire, warming them and rubbing them briskly, and turned to the youth beside him.

"You are rested?"

The youth nodded.

"Tarlene will bring us food shortly. We can use this time to talk if you wish."

"How is Jem?"

"He's fine. He'll be back on his feet in a day or so," the old man answered, massaging his eye with his hand. He looked at the hand and then at Balzan. "He seemed more worried about you than himself."

Balzan grinned. "I am fond of him also. He is one of the leaders your people need."

Taza pursed his lips. "He is an unusual young man, Balzan, that is true, but he has much to learn."

"What do you mean?"

Taza seemed uncomfortable. "He takes too many risks. Also, he is reluctant to adhere to any counsel other than his own. He persists in his belief that an antique machine will save our people."

"At least he believes in something besides being a slave," Balzan said unkindly.

Balzan got to his feet and stretched. "I am hungry."

The old man cleared his throat, pushed himself up. "Come, follow me."

Balzan ate ravenously. Tarlene sat beside him. Her eyes were bright and happy. Balzan smiled at her and she laughed back at him. Her hand touched his shoulder. "The food pleases you?"

He nodded, saying nothing. The youth's obvious enjoyment of her labors filled her with pleasure.

Taza sat and looked reflectively at Balzan as he ate.

"What's troubling you, Taza?" Balzan asked the old man.

"The Krells have been taking many reprisals these past days. Even now, airships are stalking our countryside laying waste to both Orathians and Corillians."

"Then we will give them a little more to worry about."

"Balzan," Tarlene said. She leaned forward, put her hand against his face, and said softly, "I do not want to lose you again."

Balzan placed his arm about her and she put her head on his shoulder. He looked at Taza again.

"How far is this machine that Jem puts so much faith in?"

The old man hunched his shoulders. "Not far. It is housed in a deserted compound the Krells have long ceased patrolling, but with the sudden wave of violence and the reprisals, I don't know."

"Isn't this what you've wanted? I don't understand you, Taza. You should be joyous that your people are rebelling."

"I am. I just do not want my people slaughtered in vain. Remember, Balzan, the Krells are not so ignorant that they will allow us time to mass and plan our strategy. Even now my people are being herded to the mines—or worse."

"Then we must act at once. If this machine cannot be restored, then let us formulate other plans."

"That is all well and good for you, Balzan, you to whom the word 'slavery' has a disgusting sound. But slavery has been our way of life. To eradicate it we need more than just one machine, we need numbers."

"At least the machine is a start, Taza. If the Krells know

you can fight back it will give your people a better position for bargaining."

"I don't know," the old Chronicler sighed. "Perhaps it was ordained that we should be the Krells' servants."

Balzan hung his shoulders wearily. Taza was reacting to the situation in a way that was not totally unknown to Balzan. In a sense it was the same way the Cat People had reacted when they were taken prisoner by the Kharnites.

To the Cat People, the concept of free will or of change was alien. They accepted all situations. The Endorians were not cowards, they might fight to stay alive, but never to change the way they lived. It was not part of their nature. The Orathians, a completely different race, were paralleling his adopted family in a way that bothered and angered Balzan.

It seemed that the elders were suppressing the younger men like Jem who had the will to fight. They used words, where Jem was determined to use force.

If the Orathians were to be free, it was going to have to be by force not by words. Jem realized this, yet older and wiser Taza did not. Balzan understood this, but still it annoyed him.

"What have you in mind, Taza?"

"I leave for the city soon. During the Krell feast we Chroniclers are allowed to address our people. There I was hoping to show enough strength to present our demands to Androth. Now I don't know. It appears that the Krells are totally dedicated to punishing us for our revolt."

"Then let us give them food for thought. We have started our resistance. Let us continue. First let's go to the machine, then we'll proceed accordingly."

"All right," Taza sighed, "I asked for your aid. The least I can do is give you my assistance and knowledge. Come then, it is but a short distance."

Balzan and Tarlene followed the old man through a low hatchway that led down a long, tubelike, metallic corridor. It ended in an immense room with a glass dome covering its entirety. The room abounded with metallic objects and consoles that Balzan had seen before aboard his parents' vessel. The center of the room was dominated by a huge cannon pointed upward. Behind him, Taza pushed a switch and Balzan saw red and white glowing lights emanating from the cannon.

"Where does the power come from?" Balzan asked.

The old man pointed to the dome roof. "The instruments are all powered by solar energy. Do not ask me to explain it. The Lathogauts were an enterprising race; it took the Krells many years to destroy them."

Balzan saw that one of the consoles covered an entire wall and several chairs were slung low before it beneath a large opaque screen. Balzan remembered a similar screen from his years as a student of the teacher.

"This is probably the nerve center. Have you talked to the computer?"

The old man raised an eyebrow. "I have talked to no one. As you can see there is nothing left but machinery. There is no one called Computer here."

Balzan grinned to himself. "Of course. I should have said machine."

"Machine?" Taza exclaimed.

"You will be careful, Balzan," Tarlene said with fear in her eyes. "Two of our people died by touching these things."

"I am aware of how the machines function, Tarlene," Balzan answered reassuringly.

He pushed a metal plate in front of him and the console immediately came to life. The machine hummed, and lights flashed on and off. Balzan reclined in the chair and adjusted it to his size. He pushed another plate above a row of endless buttons. The screen brightened and formed a wavering line that moved in electronic cadence across the screen. Balzan spoke to the screen as Taza and Tarlene looked at each other in bewilderment.

"Computer, I am Balzan. Do you identify with my speech pattern?"

Instantly a green button in the row of endless buttons was illuminated. Balzan pushed it and the wavering line upon the screen changed instantly into a straight line and different color. The voice from the console caused Taza and Tarlene to cringe back in terror.

YOU SPEAK IN AN ALIEN TONGUE WHICH REQUIRES THE DECH BUTTON.

Another button lit up and Balzan pushed it. The image on the screen now turned to several vertical lines.

"Can you converse with me now, computer?" Balzan asked.

AFFIRMATIVE. HOWEVER I DO NOT PROGRAM RESPONSES THAT WOULD ALTER ANY LATHO-GAUT INSTRUCTION.

"I am a comrade to the Lathogauts. I question you only in their behalf."

PLACE YOUR EXTREMITIES UPON THE PLATES TO YOUR LEFT.

"No," Tarlene screamed, "it will destroy you, Balzan."

Balzan motioned to her to be silent, then did as the computer ordered. The screen turned to a series of amber dots and then returned to the vertical lines.

HUMANOID. AGE TWENTY-ONE YEARS. BODY TEMPERATURE 98.6. VARIABLE DEGREE OF IN-TELLIGENCE. . . . INFERIOR TO LATHOGAUT CULTURE BY 38.7 MILOTREMS.

"I am also here for answers that will aid me in destroying the enemies of the Lathogauts."

IMPROBABLE STATEMENT SINCE LATHOGAUT CULTURE HAS BEEN EXTERMINATED BY ZE-TARIANS.

"I thought the Lathogauts were in combat with the Krell race, computer."

THE KRELL RACE ARE INFERIOR TO YOU BY 41.3 MILOTREMS.

Balzan turned to Taza and Tarlene who were standing in awe at what they were witnessing. Balzan pondered the answer by the computer for a moment, then pushed the plate again.

"Computer, answer my query without comment. I am the operator and you are programmed to answer."

AFFIRMATIVE.

"I ask no query that will be detrimental to the Lathogauts, but I require information. Who are the Zetarians?"

ALIEN CULTURE THAT NOW RULES KRELL CULTURE.

Balzan turned to Taza. "Have you ever heard of the Zetarians?"

The old man, visibly shaken, muttered, "The Feast of Zetar is to the god of the Krells. As for a race, I have never heard of them."

Balzan pushed the metal plate again. "Explain Zetarian culture."

NEGATIVE. CULTURE IS NOT PROGRAMMED.

ALL DATA WAS DESTROYED BY RE-PROGRAM-MING AT LAST SEMINAR BEFORE EXODUS.

"Computer," Balzan leaned forward eagerly. "Explain please."

CULTURE MATRIX INDICATOR WAS REMOVED AND RE-PROGRAMMED. SENSORS ARE ALL THAT REMAIN. HISTORICAL DATA IS AVAILABLE IF YOU REQUEST.

"I do," Balzan said impatiently.

ZETARIAN RACE HAS COMMANDED KRELL RACE FOR NINE BILEMS. THE KRELL RACE HAS ALL TECHNOLOGY GIVEN IT VIA LIGHT SENSOR IN THE TEMPLE OF ZETAR.

"How does it function, can you explain?"

NEGATIVE. POWER IS EMANATED THROUGH ONE BODY. A KRELL THAT ACTS AS HOST. THE POWER IS APPROXIMATELY SEVEN BILLION MIL-OTREMS ABOVE LATHOGAUT.

Balzan detected the same smug tone in the metallic voice that his teacher had possessed. He pressed down on the plate again. "Where are the Lathogauts now?"

RESPONSE TO QUERY IS NEGATIVE FOR OB-VIOUS REASON. ZETARIANS HAVE DESTROYED DURING THEIR EXODUS.

Balzan looked up at the screen and pondered his next question.

"Can the Zetarians be defeated?"

NEGATIVE. LATHOGAUT RACE EXTERMINAT-ED. WEAPONRY INADEQUATE TO COMBAT CERE-BRAL MIND SURGERY AND MYSTICAL TELEPOR-TATION.

"Explain."

DATA INSUFFICIENT. CAN EXPLAIN ONLY EF-FECT NOT CAUSE.

"Are the Zetarians primates similar to the Krells?"

NO DATA.

Balzan sighed. "Why do they use the Krells for their tasks?"

NO DATA.

With a sigh. Balzan removed his hand from the chair arm and swung away from the console. Tarlene rushed to him. "Balzan, the machine talked."

"Yes, I know."

"But how?"

"I have talked to other machines, Tarlene. They are made and operated by man—to serve man. Do not be frightened. Can you offer any explanation to what was said, Taza?"

"None," the Chronicler said in dismay. "I am more confused now than I have ever been. That machine said that the Krells were ruled by the Zetarians. The god Zetar is worshipped, I know, but I assumed that it was just another of their pagan images."

Balzan knew that the fact of another alien culture controlling the Krells was not impossible. Was he not an alien himself? He had grown up with the Cat People, yet he had been presented, through his teacher, knowledge that was beyond his understanding. He knew he was a man—a human—and though part of his cultural background was developed with the Endorians, he still was born of a different species. He was endowed with emotions and feelings that differed greatly from those of the races that walked the continents of the world he was upon. It troubled him, but yet it made him feel superior, stronger. He was a man who did not allow simple facts to cloud his reason. There were always two sides to a story and each race was different. No matter how repulsive or backward they appeared, they were revered by someone. For all their savagery somewhere there was kindness.

He returned to the console.

"Can the cannon be restored to its full capacity?"

AFFIRMATIVE.

"Can you explain its function to me?"

AFFIRMATIVE.

"Explain then."

YOU HAVE IT ARMED AT THIS MOMENT.

Balzan turned to the weapon. "You mean the flashing lights?"

AFFIRMATIVE. THE LIGHTS SEEN ARE PRELIMINARY TO FIRING. ONCE THE CANNON FIRES THE GLOWING EFFECT IS STOPPED.

"What happens when it is fired?"

THE CANNON FIRES A BEAM THAT BEGINS TRANSPARENT IN INTENSITY. AS IT CONTINUES IT BECOMES DEEPER AND STRONGER.

"And when it strikes a target what happens?"

THE EXPLOSION IS IMMEDIATE UPON CON-
TACT. POWER IS INCREASED BY LEVER BLUE . . .
THEN RED . . . INTENSE BEAM OBLITERATES
ANY TARGET WITHIN SENSOR READINGS. LEVER
WHITE—OPENS DOME PORTAL FOR FIRING.

"Any malfunctions I should know of?"

AFFIRMATIVE. IF CIRCUITS BEGIN TO OVER-
HEAT IT MUST BE SHUT OFF.

"Then what happens?"

WHEN CANNON IS SHUT OFF AND THE BEAM
STOPS THE METAL WILL COOL FROM WHITE HOT
TO RED TO ITS ORIGINAL METALLIC COLOR.

The computer explained the entire firing procedure. Balzan pushed the lever that opened the dome with a squeak of rusty metal. Then he pushed another lever that activated the machine's beam.

It worked.

Chapter Eight

Although the Lathogauts had perfected sophisticated weaponry, their successors were not so clever. The Orathians were not night workers and the unequal development of their society found one of its weakest spots in artificial lighting. Their lamps were poor flickering things that strained the eyes and cast only a pale yellow glow.

Balzan was amazed that he could read the detailed airship corridor maps, let alone make any sense of them.

Tarlene entered the room in which he was working. To utilize the weapon room's lights would be to invite scrutiny from a Krell patrol.

The youth sat cross-legged, the map loosely open in his lap, noting and marking. Tarlene had never met such a man before and she held the youth in awe. Balzan was a leader. To her people he was their champion. A leader in peace and a leader in war was still a constant of the old legends, and in the days of old many Orathians had possessed the qualities of courage that Balzan had. But those were old days that Tarlene had long since forgotten.

Even before she had closed the door behind her, Balzan nodded for her to seat herself on the bed, a matter of necessity, since there was no other comfortable space to sit in the room—and then he went on with his work. She closed the door and sat down on the bed.

She watched his intense young face trying to decipher the maps in the dim light. She sat quietly for a while, then asked, "What are you reading?"

He looked at her inquiringly. The request was perfunctory, a conversational opening. It was evident Tarlene was bored.

"You wouldn't understand."

"Yes I would. If you explained it to me."

"I'm having a difficult time explaining it to myself," he

stated modestly.

"Is it interesting?" she asked in childlike innocence.

"Not interesting, but sad," Balzan answered seriously, looking at the woman gravely and steadily. "The Krells have an impressive military routine. Every corner of Orathia and Corillia is patroled by their airships. The Lathogauts were a highly advanced race and yet they were completely destroyed."

"Perhaps they angered the Lord Androth," Tarlene said smiling.

Tarlene was a puzzlement to Balzan. He could conclude that the Krells were a vindictive people, stern and power-hungry. But Tarlene not only accepted them but actually felt that by her slavery the Krells were only invoking the necessity of justice. To explain that, even to himself, Balzan tried to grasp the logic of that justice. He could. But could not grasp the acceptance of it by the beautiful woman before him.

There definitely was some type of mass brain-control operating on the Orathians, and somehow it all stemmed from the mountain that housed the god Zetar. Balzan had gained much information from the Lathogaut computer. It seemed the odds were highly improbable of success against the Krells.

"Balzan, can't you talk to me for a while? I'm so very lonesome," Tarlene said, placing her hand on his arm.

"Shortly, Tarlene. I want to finish this so I can explain it with some sense of accuracy to Taza."

"All right," she smiled, "but only if you promise to walk with me later."

He nodded and returned to the charts. He worked with them for another half hour then, rubbing his eyes, tossed them to the floor.

"You are very weary, Balzan," she said with concern.

"No," he replied, "I'm just bewildered by it all, Tarlene."

"I have faith in you. I know you will help my people."

"Maybe I can't, Tarlene."

She shook her head. "If you cannot no one can."

Balzan wanted her to understand, he wanted her to know and accept that there were no gods, no invincible warriors with shields of invulnerability. Her entire life had been as a slave. The Krells depended for their empire's growth on the passiveness of their conquests. The history of the Krell race had been written in warfare and blood. At first there was the continuing, unending war between themselves and the races that they had enslaved. A silent war, a war of hatred and reprisal. Then, with the appearance of Androth, the slave races became servile and complacent. But a new monster had been created—the power of an alien force controlling the warlord factions and expanding the terror to new dimensions by its sophisticated weaponry.

"Don't place all your trust in me, Tarlene. I'm no more a man than your brother Jem or any other man who hates slavery."

"You frighten me," said Tarlene. "Do you know how much I love you?"

Balzan nodded and looked searchingly at her. She was moved to cover his hand with hers, and she felt a sense of longing and warmth for him that was painful to the extreme. Here was a young man, not too much older than herself, who was deeply concerned with the fate and future of her people. It reminded her of the stories she had heard of the old times, vaguely remembered stories of her childhood, when the Orathians were a happy and productive race.

Balzan began to stroke her hand gently, and then he leaned over and kissed her. Vividly, now, she recalled the tokens of punishment, the starved bodies of her people, the horrible flashes of pain that derived from the threat of the caron. Tarlene had made a rationale of it, but now she was beginning to react differently.

"We were once a people with a great capacity for love and justice, Balzan, and I will gladly die to see that come about once more."

"I know that. And I also know that the strong qualities in you are fighting to get out, just like the Orathians that rebel now. Together we'll succeed."

He pulled her to him.

He felt, as he began to make love to Tarlene, that here was a woman who truly loved him and would die for him. Yet that did not lessen the sense of power the conquest of her afforded him. Balzan forgot momentarily the Krells, their weapons, and the futility of war as he was engulfed with the abandonment and consuming passion that gripped Tarlene. She clung to him with a desperation that took his breath. The power of his loins seemed to blend into her softness until they were a single body and spirit.

* * *

The airship *Syla* was a cylinder about sixty feet long, with a sumptuously appointed cabin taking up the aft third of the length. This was Commander Muros' flagship; it was cruising in Orathia.

The luxury of the cabin was suited to his rank. It was furnished in a sybaritic design that matched his character. Muros was reclining in his quarters sipping wine when a call came down the tube to him.

The border of Orathia had been passed and they were heading in for a landing at the Corillian village of Arle. This was the largest of the Corillian settlements. At one time the village was the prized commonwealth of the Lathogauts. Now it was part of the Krell empire.

At Arle, over the northwestern border, lay the village against the barren lands stretching away to the Pinnacles.

There were few lakes in the area, the ground was thin and sorry, and the wind scoured the landscape into wild and fantastic shapes. The Corillians were used primarily in the mines and Muros had decided to transport fresh slaves back to the capital. Now that he had laid siege to Orathia he could leave this desolation and return to Manator in a day's time.

Muros went on deck as his vessel slanted down for a landing. Across to the east where the sun rose in a jumbled blaze of scarlet and emerald the morning sky was a mass of glorious color. Clouds puffed into spirals and divided the rising beams of the sun, thus sending its glow across the horizon.

"Will you want breakfast before departing, sir?" his aide inquired.

Muros didn't bother to reply. He just stood there watching the glory of the dawn. His aide asked again and Muros nodded.

Corillia was a pleasant enough place in spots. The landing site here was abundant with vegetation, shade trees, and the soothing sounds of water trickling from an adjacent brook.

The usual amount of curious Corillians were on hand to see the giant ship gracefully set its ponderous body down into a clearing at the edge of the village.

Muros ordered his aide to notify his other ships to rendezvous at Arle, and that a hundred Corillians would be transported to the mines.

The sun was rising now, the air growing warmer. A cohort strode down the bridge parapet and took positions guarding the vessel.

Muros ordered another cohort to search the village for weapons and to check the deserted Lathogaut compound for any hiding Orathians.

Then the commander returned to his cabin for his morning meal. It would take at least the balance of the morning to herd together the new mine workers.

* * *

Balzan tossed and turned in his sleep, muttering words that were completely alien to Tarlene.

She sat by him as he slept, kept awake by his moans and his frantic talking in his sleep. He talked of a great many things. Albs, Kharnites, Aere, all words that held no meaning to Tarlene. Then he screamed in his sleep.

When that happened she woke him, for the nightmare he had been living in his sleep was impossible for her to endure any longer. She awakened him and made love to him tenderly, stroking his brow and kissing his wet skin. Tarlene remembered that when she had been a little girl, good things happened to men and women when they loved each other. That love cast out fear, the spirits and demons of the forest, and made them strong. But after Androth had made her people slaves, she had forgotten such memories and the prime instinct of her existence had become blind obedience.

Now her whole being, her existence, her living and functioning, the motion of her blood, and the beating of her heart were fused into love for the man beside her. Now she knew that the experience of men and women in the past was very true and very real.

She was no longer afraid. She was cloaked in magic, the magic of her love was real. At the same time she hoped that he loved her as well. He was a man that she loved easily, he was strong and yet he had feelings for others.

Even in this time of terrible and desperate acts he was strong. Tarlene knew of the lost souls whom the mines had destroyed, of races like the Lathogauts that had simply vanished, yet with Balzan she strangely and comfortably felt that now she could endure. He was the only man who had ever possessed her. For a time she had believed the desire in her loins was dead, but she had only to touch him to want him.

Now her hands quieted him, and she asked him, "What were you dreaming?"

He shook his head.

"Hold me close to you and you won't dream anymore."

He held her close to him and whispered to her, "Did I wake you?"

"No, I was watching you."

"Was I shouting?"

"No. Don't ever leave me, Balzan."

"What would you do if I did?" he asked her.

"I would die," she answered simply and directly.

"Don't say that," he said, awake from his dream now and calm again.

"Why should we talk of that anyway? Wherever you go I shall follow. I love you and without you I would die."

"No, Tarlene. If you loved me, you would not want to die."

"Do you think that way?"

"Yes."

"And if I died, you would not want to die?" she asked.

"I would want to live."

"Why?"

"Because there is nothing without life."

"I don't understand."

"Not at this moment, perhaps. But someday you will, Tarlene."

Finally she said, "I won't think of death now. There is too much to live for."

Then, in a little while, he was asleep, calmly and gently, with her arms around him.

A Corillian's message that the Krell airship was in the village brought Taza racing to Balzan.

"How many?" Balzan asked.

"A cohort," the old man gasped.

"Will they come here?"

"I don't know. Fiala said they were herding together men for the mines. Jem was one of those taken."

"No," Tarlene shrieked.

Balzan put his arm around her. "Don't worry, we'll get him back. How long will the ship stay at the village?"

The old man shrugged. "Until they have a full cargo, I would expect."

"Then we will move quickly," Balzan said, getting to his feet and sheathing his sword. The older man stopped him.

"Wait, Balzan, there probably is a chance that more ships are on the way. Usually a flagship does not transport slaves."

The youth retrieved his charts and studied them. He looked up at Taza with a twinkle in his eye. "Good, there's also a chance since they're coming from Orathia they will come in range of our cannon."

"But I thought we would use the device only as an instrument to bargain with."

Balzan's eyes hardened. "Those men being herded for the mines haven't got time for talk, Taza."

The older man nodded in agreement and followed Balzan to the compound where the cannon waited.

The Corillian messenger watched the youth walk confidently to the compound. His face went through a whole spectrum of expressions, from dumb animal wonder to a glorious sunrise of hope.

"They are coming!" announced Taza.

Balzan looked out across the rolling country in the direction of the village and presently he saw, from his vantage point in the dome, the advance of a Krell patrol.

Balzan pushed the lever and the dome opened. He activated the cannon and set it in motion on the target. For a moment he could make nothing out of what he saw through the range finder. The screen seemed to be billowing with a green substance. Then it cleared. Teeth clenched, Balzan watched the crosshairs on the screen creep with infinite slowness toward the approaching and unwary Krells.

He shot a glance at Tarlene, who was standing pale and terrified. Taza, grim-faced, nodded in assent with Balzan.

Balzan nodded back and moved his fingers over the instruments. He hit the firing lever once with his hand.

The light flashed.

The Krell patrol vanished.

With the success of the weapon Balzan returned to the computer. He needed more answers. The computer seemed reluctant to activate but soon the screen flickered again.

"Computer, you have told me your data has been terminated on Zetarians. But your memory bank sensors must retain some data. Is this true?"

The horizontal line on the screen changed to a series of dots. The metallic voice once again came forward.

ALL BACK INFORMATION RETAINED CANNOT AID IN ANY ENDEAVOR TO CONQUER SAME.

"I'm aware of this, computer. I want only pertinent data that affected Lathogauts and now Orathians."

INSUFFICIENT DATA ONLY ALLOWED TO . . .

"Cancel," Balzan said. "I repeat, answer only my questions that are still in your memory banks. Is that understood?"

AFFIRMATIVE.

"What is Zetar?"

NO DATA.

"Who is Zetar?"

NO DATA.

"Computer, I wish to carry on Lathogaut technology. I cannot do so without your aid. What alternatives can you offer me in learning of the force that eliminated your creators!"

NO DATA.

"You have some data on Lathogaut procedures learned."

INSUFFICIENT FOR ANY PURPOSE.

Balzan was getting nothing from the machine. He switched several buttons on the memory circuit. When he depressed the reprogram button the machine came alive.

CHANNEL INPUT NOW READY FOR EXPLANATION TO SEVER LAST DATA IN MEMORY BANKS.

Balzan realized that the Krells had overlooked completely erasing the computer's stored memory. In its perfection of design the computer now was awaiting total cancellation of its memory process in relationship to the Zetarians.

The questions would be answered and then erased. The computer in essence would be destroyed with each syllable. Balzan needed the vital information it held. He pressed the plate again. The machine's console swirled in a series of lines and colors. It was ready to die.

"Computer, explain terminology of Zetar."

The screen altered color and a mathematical formula appeared on the viewer.

$$Ff^2 (MgE) - C^1 R^1 \times M = L/so$$

"Explain audio."

ZETAR ONE PROBE ON THIS WORLD TWENTY BILLION SPECTS ALL PROGRAMMING COMPLETE.

"Cancel. Explain mathematics displayed, not origin."

THE ZETAR PROBE IS ONE OF THREE THOUSAND SENTRIES DISPLACED IN GALAXY FOR RECORDING OF LIFE FUNCTIONS. NUMBER OF STARS IN UNIVERSE IS SO INFINITE THAT ONLY ONE IN BILLION HAS SUN WITH PLANETS.

"What is their purpose?"

INVESTIGATION OF ALIEN LIFE FORMS AND SOCIAL SYSTEMS.

"Does their programming allow them to assist the culture of this world or to annihilate and enslave others?"

ANY REQUIRED ASSISTANCE TO LIFE FORM IS ALLOWED AS LONG AS THEY ARE FED KNOWLEDGE.

"How?"

BY DIGESTING IN COMPUTER BANKS OXYGEN-CARBON LIFE FORM SUPPLIED BY ALIEN SERVANT.

"You mean the men who worked the mines were fed to them?"

ONLY THEIR INTELLECT VIA CEREBRAL THOUGHT TRANSFER.

"What purpose did that satisfy a machine that was not of flesh and blood?"

ALL PROGRAMMING AND STIMULI ARE ACCEPTABLE TO MAINTAIN DATA FOR ZETARIAN.

"For what?" Balzan realized he was shouting at a machine and composed himself.

THEIR MASTERS HAVE DECREED THAT KNOWLEDGE OF THIS WORLD BE DIGESTED AND RELAYED TO THEM WHEN THEY RETURN.

"How did they reach Androth and supply him with such power?"

ANDROTH—KRELL RULER. NEEDED YOUTH TO BUILD FORCES. SUPPLIED MUCH STIMULI.

Balzan understood that the method of communicating language was simplified by the establishment of a telecommunicator that converted all alien language into English or whatever language addressed the computer. Androth, in his ignorance, thought it was a god. He wasn't even aware that the Lathogauts had also developed computers.

This computer was simplified and basic. It was armed with a self-protection beam and generated intense light as a throw-off power beam. What disgusted Balzan was a life form that had created a machine that required human nourishment. The Zetarians obviously were a race long dead, but their faithful computers that fed on brain waves for stimuli still existed, and they still performed their function day after day, year after year, eon after eon. With all their intelligence and imagination they had forgotten one small factor. Balzan knew the factor. The Zetarians had believed in only their culture. They never discovered or sought to discover that the differences in cultures, of ideas and attitudes, are stimuli in themselves. What makes life and exploration exciting is variety. It is an infinite delight. The Zetarians considered all other cultures savage. That probably was their downfall. Balzan did not know, or care, for that matter.

"Where is the planet Zetar?"

INACCURATE TERMINOLOGY. ZETAR ENCOMPASSES ENTIRE SOLAR SYSTEM.

"Are computers included?"

YES. ONCE PROGRAMMED, PROGRAMMING IS INFINITE.

"Can it malfunction?"

CONCEPT WEAK. AS ZETARIAN MATHEMATICS WITHOUT FLAW ALL DATA STORED IS INFINITE.

"All data?"

AFFIRMATIVE.

"Last question, computer. Can the Zetarians be fallible in any degree?"

NEGATIVE.

Balzan switched off the machine and slumped in his chair. He was curious to see a creature that was infallible. Even though the computer was programmed to believe so, Balzan doubted what he was told.

In any event, he would soon see for himself.

Chapter Nine

Commander Muros strolled across a little river, relaxing while his men gathered the slaves. The bridge was a Lathogaut bridge of heavy stone, worn by the floods and trampling of many years. He let the breeze refresh him and thought of Emor and his displeasure.

Before Emor, he had played the suppliant to gain slaves for Manator; he had strained every nerve to keep his name in the Forum circles. He was ambitious and he had seen at once how powerful Emor was. He joined his service, because to rise he needed Emor's support—guidance and direction.

Like Emor, the shrewd Muros had no illusions and he knew the citizens of Manator. There the similarity ended, for Muros had no resources other than his agile, stubborn brain, his sword, and the admiration of his followers.

He could keep his own counsel. He turned his back on any policy except the policy Emor desired. Ambition smoldered in him, feeding his hunger for new glory.

Around him now stretched rolling hills, grazing Stayktons, a deserted governor's tower, and a decrepit village.

His men came past with Corillians destined for the mines in tow. The jangle of chains and the cracking of whips disturbed his meditation. He moved back toward his ship. His other two vessels would arrive soon and he would transport the slaves back to the city.

By reporting, order had been restored and his mission made successful. He hoped to regain Emor's shaken confidence. Muros took no pity on the Corillian village.

While half of his men corralled the mine slaves, the other half were dispensing Krell justice.

The warriors were beating the older, unarmed men. They

pulled the women from the huts, flung them down, and violated them. The screaming of children, the sobbing and hysterical shrieks of the struggling women shrilled above the morning air.

Muros was oppressed by longing and a dream. Fair indeed was Manator, with its rich valleys, wide stone-flagged streets, and magnificent structures, but he longed to create a new province that Emor had pondered assigning him. Now he might be chastised for letting the Monitor trick him.

Emor was planning to invade Quito. Quito was a desired province for the Krells and he, Muros, knew how to hold it. He also knew exactly what allies the Krells would have in taking it, and how the frontiers could be guarded and extended. And, until his blunder, he had already laid plans as the first Governor of Quito.

He returned to his ship and passed the time awaiting his fleet by consuming more wine than he should have.

* * *

Balzan calibrated the cannon at its full magnification. At first his target score showed nothing but a scan of clouds, then the two approaching airships were there. These would be the slave carriers bound for rendezvous with their flagship.

Balzan put the crosshairs on the lead ship. He judged its distance, but its size was impossible to guess. He pushed his lever to full intensity. The lights flashed and the beam exploded the unwary ship in a burst of orange flame.

It plummeted to the ground in a mass of black smoke and fire.

The second vessel altered its course and moved toward the compound. Balzan sighted the ship through the score; it was gaining altitude but was still approaching the compound.

Taza pointed mutely, and Balzan nodded. At close range the Krell vessel looked like a bird of prey with halfspread wings. Balzan blinked and leaned forward tensely, resetting the range.

The Krell ship launched a torpedo bolt of blinding light from its underbelly. The incendiary blast jarred the compound. Moving with deliberateness, as if it were traveling in slow motion, it fired again. The blast hit so close that it seemed to engulf the compound.

The mass in motion fired again at the same instant that Balzan squeezed the lever. The compound was in flames. Balzan, crawling on his hands and knees, saw that Taza had spirited Tarlene to safety. He limped from the building and fell at a safe distance just as the structure blew up.

His eyes darted to the sky, and a triumphant smile drew across his features as he saw the Krell ship plunging to the ground in flames; upon impact it exploded into a fiery ball of red that sent black smoke billowing into the sky.

* * *

The viewscreen of Muros' flagship spat static through the central room. The speaker squawked desperately and went dead.

"Prepare for battle," Muros told his aide very quietly. "We have lost our fleet. Signal the warriors to leave the slaves and board immediately."

Muros raised his right fist over the plot board, still clenched. The knuckles and tendons worked for a moment. Then he smashed it down savagely. "No, I will not run like a frightened animal.

"Prepare defenses to repel boarders. Assemble our remaining troops in a wedge around the vessel. We will fight —to the death, if need be."

His aide turned to him, his lips quivering. "The slaves, sir, are charging the vessel."

He motioned to his armor captain. The man pushed two buttons and intense rays of white light covered the area in front of the ship. At least twenty Corillians screamed and fell to the ground, charred beyond recognition from the heat.

"This isn't a battle," Muros said, "nor even a skirmish. It's Krells against animals. Signal Manator for information on any other vessels in the area."

The aide pounded up to the bridge. There, on the communications board, a strange muted gabble was issuing, fading in and out, and hashed with static. The aide turned the knob, but could only receive a weak signal. It was modulated and impossible to arrange to send a message.

But nothing happened, then a channel cleared and the

83

aide gave his distress signal, but the response was of high impedance and he was not sure that the message had been received.

Muros appeared above him.

"I don't know if they received it, sir."

"Send it again," Muros ordered.

A warrior approached him. "Our beams are growing weak, sir. Should we use our turrets only on boarding attempts?"

"Yes, use them," Muros declared promptly. "Save the beams for a mass attack."

He then whirled to face the terrible clamor outside. The Corillians were plunging toward the ship flailing their arms, brandishing swords, and screaming murderously.

Muros, moved by some obscure impulse, pressed the beam lever again, sending a shower of death at the attacking mob.

There was a dull spatter in the still air. The beam's power was gone. The plaintive sound was answered instantly by almost thunderous screams of rage.

"Forward turrets, fire," he commanded.

The sounds of exploding fireballs burst into the air and the attackers darted for cover. The ground squad was locked in close combat now, sword to sword.

Jem was in the thick of the battle, his blade moving swiftly and accurately. The Krells were outnumbered fifty to one, yet they stood and fell in blind loyalty.

Muros, for a fleeting second, weighed the thought of slicing his mooring lines and escaping. Instead, he drew his sword and clambered down the rope ladder to join his warriors in the skirmish.

Balzan and his companions reached the scene of battle just as Jem's blade severed the head of the last ground reserve. Now the decks were lined and ready with Krell warriors awaiting the final onslaught. They were over twenty feet above the villagers and had the advantage of killing many before their defenses were breached.

The boarding and landing tackle was tethered beneath the keel, a mass of cordage and leather. Balzan saw that it was moored by at least four cables. Escape was now impossible for the Krells if he could prevent the lines from being cut.

There was not an instant of hesitation. Swinging like a

bob on a pendulum he climbed the cables. Catching one leg on the deck rail he pulled himself aboard. One of the Krells spotted him and rushed to confront him.

Drawing his sword he dodged the descending blade. Balzan, in a crouched position, drove his blade deep into the chest.

Balzan went into action with blurring speed. His sword flashed. He struck furiously with a crash and the helmet and head of another Krell were cloven to the chin. Several turned to him. Seeing their vessel boarded brought them at a mad lunge toward him.

Balzan kicked the corpse against the others, breaking their charge, while dodging a cut aimed at his legs by one who had evaded the body flung at them.

With a terrific backhanded swipe, he cut the sword arm from the man's body. The arm fell to the deck, while its owner sank down in a heap.

Jem and several others were now boarding, but they were met with heavy resistance.

Balzan stormed against the two flanking him. With flashing blades, they fought for their lives under the maddened onslaught of the enraged youth. Fury blazed in his eyes as he rained stroke after stroke upon their frantic parries, circling them to keep them at the deck. He saw one attempt to leap over the side.

Balzan's blade flickered like a shaft of light. A terrific slash sheared off the head of the escaping Krell. With the savageness of the blow the other backed against the rail.

Their swift blows and parries blended into a pattern of steel.

Tarlene, watching from below, cried out in terror as Balzan slipped in the blood on the deck and fell back over the decapitated corpse.

The Krell sprang forward, triumph in his eyes. He raised his sword. Balzan struggled to rise. Suddenly, the mouth of the Krell flew open. He teetered, dropped his sword, and fell with a choking gurgle. Standing behind him was the grinning figure of Jem.

Balzan rose, covered with blood, but his blue eyes blazed with unquenchable fire.

"Lucky you were quicker than I. Once again you have saved me."

"To kill Krells," Jem roared. "Let's finish the job."

Muros fought on like a man possessed. There was no escape; the alternatives were death or surrender. Muros' mind hung undecided, not knowing what to do, but his hands fought mindlessly. As a Corillian blade came at him, he dipped, swung his sword sharply, and drove it aside. He fought without involvement, his body moving by reflex.

He heard the clatter of steel on both sides of him and saw his sword enter the man's ribs. As in a daze, he bolted inside the ship and down to his spacious cabin. Balzan saw the commander, his bloody sword in the sunlight, disappear inside and followed him.

He turned to see Muros lunge and parried the blow. Muros lashed out and kicked the youth in the groin, sending him backward.

As Balzan spun away he lifted his sword to fend off another thrust that was coming straight at his throat.

His sword flashed at the elbow and the Krell commander was screaming at his feet. Balzan watched the raw horror of the man's agony reach a piercing scream. He stopped the scream with a thrust through the commander's chest.

Jem's face appeared. "We've won. They're defeated. There's only one Krell left alive. We've won."

* * *

At Balzan's appearance on deck the villagers cheered him in triumph. He descended the ladder and Tarlene rushed to his arms.

She embraced him hotly, straining with her vigorous, slim, young body against his, covering his lips with kisses until his senses reeled. He shook his head and thrust her gently from him. He held her at arms's length.

The lone survivor of the Krell forces was thrown at Balzan's feet. "Spare me," he cried.

"Kill him, Balzan," the crowd roared. He silenced them with a wave of his hand.

"No. He will deliver our words to the Krells. Words they will long remember."

The Krell trembled in fear, clutching his wound and avoiding Balzan's eyes.

"From this moment on the Orathians and Corillians are no longer slaves."

Then Balzan's voice was drowned out by the joyful shouts of the crowd that had gathered around him. With a sudden inner strength he accepted the humble adoration of these people whose sole hope of freedom he represented.

Chapter Ten

Daylight brings no cheer to a condemned man. To great men, daylight washes away the confusions of the night. Great men assume the mantle of their greatness anew each morning. After a night of bitter news Emor, protector of Manator, Counsel Warrior, felt less than great.

Sitting on his terrace, mantled in a fresh snow-white tunic with his gold insignia and gold trappings, his face a façade of confidence and superiority, Emor was the picture of what a great conqueror should be. It was true that he was born the son of a merchant and that the blood in his veins was of dubious ancestry, but he was very rich, and it was a virtue of the Krells that a man was measured in terms of himself at least as much as in terms of his ancestors. The very fact that Androth had chosen him as fleet counsel was an indication of his inborn qualities. He had conquered all of the Slazon Empire in one campaign, restored order in the provinces of the reptile barbarians that called themselves Morks, brought the Corillians and Orathians to their knees, and completely eradicated the once-powerful Lathogauts. He knew his limitations well, for he knew all too wisely that his riches and power remained only as long as he remained in Androth's favor.

Androth's own daughter was his mistress and his only rival for the Krell citizens' favor was the Monitor, an instrument of power that Androth held in as high esteem as he did himself. Yet Emor knew that Lenor, to whom the throne would pass in time, despised the old political wizard as much as he did. Emor knew that Lenor would select him as her next mate and in time he and he alone would rule Manator.

But this morning, as protocol demanded, he must stand

before the Monitor and answer for his protégé Muros, who had disgraced his service and dishonored the Empire.

Emor could see the old Monitor, outwardly sympathetic, expounding on Emor's past glories to the Forum. But inwardly he was relishing every humiliating moment.

Emor was content to bide his time. He summoned his servant for his cloak and prepared for the siege ahead.

The guards lifted their swords, Emor gave them a sketchy salute, rapped out his orders, and started for the palace.

The fresh air left him feeling alert and breezy, even though the past night had left fatigue beginning to creep along his bones.

He climbed through the crowded streets and along wide boulevards where Orathians toiled on the beautification of the city. Below, men toiled in the mines, always increasing the wealth of Androth.

There were few boats in the harbor and only one airship on patrol. Birds swooped and gyrated in the sun.

Around to the eastern face of the palace he strode beneath the frowning walls where the elite guard paced. In through a square opening, faced with marble and gold, then up again along courtyards where exotic birds chirped and shrilled in their jeweled cages. Past the colonnade where the magnificent chimaro reclined. Its sleek body and intense eyes were riveted on all those who passed.

Emor strode past the palace pet without a second glance as it contentedly groomed its yellow and black fur to a sheen.

Emor stalked into the Forum chambers. Removing his gold plumed helmet he saluted his rival, the Monitor.

It was a huge room with sun filtering from all directions from its domed roof. The rays cast weird gleams upon the statues of mythical birds and beasts. The doors closed behind him. Seated on the dais around him were the august body of the Forum—twenty of Manator's most distinguished citizens.

The Forum sat in whole session; only one or two chairs were empty. Emor remembered many sessions held during crises. He decided that at times of crisis and bitter knowledge the Forum was at its best. Emor took his seat. The eyes of the old men who sat so silent were full of consequence and without troubled fear, but the faces of the younger men were hard and angry.

But all of them were acutely conscious of the dignity of Emor, and within that context he felt superior. He knew these men, he knew that inwardly they feared him and their words would be tempered. He was not here to give excuses for his aide's failure, he was here to offer solutions.

There was no time to gloat over his own personal triumphs. They were inseparable from what he faced. He felt sorrow for Muros, but he cast aside his grief and petty retribution.

The Monitor rose and extended his arm. "In the name of our supreme Master, Androth, I call these citizens of Manator to order. Let the Forum open. I call upon Inquisitor Berta to begin the proceedings."

With a polite nod to Emor he sat again. The old Krell Berta stood in the center and directed his comments to the seated Forum.

"Commander Muros of the fleet of Emor under pledge to his Forum undertook the minor task of restoring order in the provinces of Orathia and Corillia. His pledge was to discipline the people and dispatch the assassins of Chalak, the slain governor."

The Monitor's eyes darted to Emor who sat listening impassively to the old Krell's oratory laced with attempts at eloquence and irritability at Emor's failure.

"Upon leaving Orathia to gather mine slaves at Corillia he lost three of Manator's finest vessels and over sixty Krell warriors. A lone survivor, Riam, is present to relate the tragic events."

The doors opened and a Krell warrior stood facing them. He was furtive, frightened; one eye twitched and his tongue anxiously licked his lips again and again. He was tired and had been wounded; a blood-soaked bandage covered his shoulder. The man stood at attention. It was only on such an occasion that he had ever been allowed into the Forum. To the warrior this was the arm and authority of Manator.

Berta began his formal questioning.

"Your name?"

"Riam."

"Riam?"

"Riam of Lord Emor's fleet," the warrior repeated.

The warrior looked from face to face, the rows of stolid,

white-tunicked men, the stone seats in which they sat like graven images. He licked his lips again. His eyes fell on Emor's and with a look of fear and shame he lowered his eyes.

"I want you to answer each question. I want all the facts that you can relate. Is that understood?"

The man nodded his head.

"Who was your commander?"

"Muros."

"Now I desire you to tell me and the Forum assembled here exactly what happened at Corillia. Tell me directly and clearly. The Monitor does not hold any blame to you. In this sacred chamber nothing will harm you."

It was not easy for the warrior to talk coherently. Emor raged inwardly, *Instead of terrifying this warrior they should get to the business of chastising me.* He rose and addressed the Monitor.

"Lord Monitor, I am sure the Forum is aware of the events. Can we not dismiss this man and I will answer all charges?"

The Monitor smiled and spoke reverently and respectfully. But there was contempt in his words. "Lord Emor, we do not wish to degrade your warrior and I understand your concern. However, if I am to report to Androth I must be aware of the firsthand information."

Emor sat down in disgust and placed a hand upon his forehead. It was clear the Monitor had no intention of sparing him one moment's degradation.

"Continue," the Monitor commanded.

The flat words of the frightened unimaginative warrior continued with the testimony.

"The Orathians and Corillians had banded together a hideous machine that blew our airships from the sky. Commander Muros located the source and destroyed the shelter with incendiary missiles. But it was too late. The savages attacked the flagship that was moored."

"Go on," Berta prodded.

Here the warrior groped for speech. He looked as if he were going to faint but he did not. "Then Commander Muros and the remaining two cohorts were slaughtered."

The Forum chamber held such a silence that the warrior's strained breath was loud and heavy.

"Go on."

"I drew my sword and dashed into the battle. I cut at one of the enemy and he disarmed me and wounded me in the side. I fell in my own blood and lay there. Then hands grasped me and pulled me to my feet. I tried to strike with my caron but he knocked it out of my hand, and there was no strength in it from the wound.

"Orathians held me with a blade an inch from my throat. Then one strode up and they all rallied around him."

"Was he the leader?"

"Yes."

"What was he called?" Berta asked.

"Balzan."

Emor saw the Monitor flinch and his eyes narrow. Emor grinned inwardly. The old fool was in trouble now as well. This was the youth that had escaped him and the same youth that Lenor had put a price upon.

The warrior continued. "I was allowed to live to return and tell the Forum that Orathians and Corillians would no longer be slaves. They would gladly embrace the Krells as equals but would fight to the death before remaining slaves. And also that until peace was attained, every Krell sighted would be destroyed."

This he said without emotion, in a straightforward manner, but his eye kept twitching and he never looked at Emor, who sat with such a grave face.

Now there was a change in the Forum, almost imperceptible but there nevertheless. They listened with hatred and tension. Now the name of Balzan came to life.

He became known from the lips of a warrior who had survived only for the purpose of having him return to the Forum and tell them of the revolt.

"Did this Balzan say anything else of importance?"

"He said to tell your Krell dogs that they have made a mockery of life. That men are worked to death in mines and that the Krell race was a race of parasites feeding on the flesh and blood of people too weak and ignorant to resist."

"Is that all?"

"His last words were a puzzlement. He said that soon the Krells would not have another culture leading them and they would have to fight with their own wits instead of an alien intelligence."

His words were heard by the Forum, their faces like

stone. The warrior was dismissed and Berta seated himself. The Monitor, now also in a position of blame, decided to change tactics.

"Men of Manator, you have heard the tale of an injured and clearly shaken warrior. I am confident that if Master Androth were present he would find it hard to control himself from laughter."

Hate flashed into Emor's eyes and he leaped to his feet. "Are you implying that my warrior falsely told the events that happened?"

"Not in the least, Lord Emor," the Monitor cooed. "It is the words that were given to him by this Balzan. Surely you, the great conqueror, servant of Androth, do not fear such threats?"

The Monitor was using flattery on Emor and it provoked him. "I fear any force that destroys my vessels and my friend."

"Yes, I also mourn Muros' passing, he was a gallant warrior. Tribute will be paid to him during the feast. However, he was defeated by a band of slaves and never before in the history of Manator has this happened."

"Let us clear the air, Lord Monitor," Emor rasped. "I take full responsibility for my aide's actions. But let me remind you—all of you—that it was in my absence that he was dispatched to Orathia."

"Are you questioning the Forum's decisions, Lord Emor?"

"Yes," Emor said defiantly. "I know that Androth would never have permitted an appointed commander of Manator's garrison to be shuttled off after rebelling savages."

The Monitor spit back at Emor, his huge jutting forehead creased with lines of anger. "It is always enlightening, Lord Emor, to see how casually you place the blame upon others. The decision of the Forum is never to be questioned. I, and I alone, follow the dictates of Androth. He was in holy retreat and I approved of the action."

"I will be glad to present this to the master when he returns. Until then I have stated that I am willing to pay the price for the failure; my sword and fleet are at your command."

The Monitor, composed now, spoke in his same soothing manner, issuing each syllable like velvet. "The Forum places no blame on its most valiant counsel. And we are grateful that you pledge the sword that has served Manator so magnificently." He swept the Forum with his eyes and was silent for a moment.

"The ritual of the Chroniclers will be terminated. All Orathians and Corillians in unlawful assembly during the feast will be slain. All Chroniclers will be imprisoned until a trial is convened." He paused and his gaze flickered to Emor.

"Fleet counsel Emor, do you accept the charge of the Forum to seek out and destroy this Balzan and his followers?"

Emor rose and answered stoically.

"I do."

"Also to lay waste to the offending provinces in the glory of our master's name even to the point of your own life?"

"I do."

The Monitor turned to Berta. "As the pledger of the Forum you have the honor of the command."

The old Krell labored to his feet, bowed to the Monitor, then to Emor. He turned to the Forum, his back straight, his eyes eager.

"The Forum must do two things. First, confirm Emor as permanent Commander of the forces of Manator."

The Forum cheered.

"Second, dispatch two fleets to intercept and destroy Balzan at the province of Orathia."

The Forum walls echoed with resounding and thunderous cheers.

As soon as Emor had departed the Forum chambers, a servant of Lenor approached him. He followed her to the Princess of the Krells' private apartments.

She awaited him with a goblet of wine. He gently brushed her lips with his. He was annoyed and in no mood for pleasantries.

"You are troubled, Lord Emor?"

He glared at her. "The old fool has succeeded again. Now I, too, depart for Orathia."

"You seem afraid."

"Afraid?" he roared. "Did you summon me here for petty games?"

She flinched. His words were tantamount to striking her across the face. She put her hands to her breast. She wore a long silver gown that fell to the floor and that was held over her shoulders by a mass of jewels.

She managed to speak. "How dare you speak to the daughter of Androth in that manner? I . . ."

She lifted her hand to strike him. He grabbed her wrist and glared down into her eyes. Her face altered in contour, to pain and then to sadness at her lover's brutality.

"Emor," she whispered. He took her in his arms and her warmth broke down his resistance and abated his anger.

He turned from her and drained his wine goblet. She watched him and rubbed her wrist.

"The Monitor, does he rule or does your father?" he asked in a hateful and harsh voice.

"You need not ask that. Androth is the only leader."

"For all you know he could be dead at this moment. No one can enter the mountain save him. How do we know he is alive?"

"If he is not, then I will rule Manator," she said proudly, "and you will sit at my side."

"And the Monitor will feel my sword at his throat."

She nodded and touched his arm. "Manator will be yours to do with as you wish, my darling, if my father is dead. The law is clear. I shall be Queen. And as Queen I can name my King."

"In the meantime I must journey to Orathia to ferret out this rabble-rouser Balzan."

Lenor's eyes widened. "Balzan? Do you mean he was part of the mob that killed Muros?"

"Part? He was the leader," Emor scoffed. "Instead of being in the city during the feast I will be searching the forests for a pack of dogs."

"Kill them, Emor, especially that youth. Bring me his head to feed to my pet."

Emor refilled his glass and slumped on Lenor's settee. "I will bring you the head of Orathia itself."

He drank more wine. Lenor unclasped her silvery robe and let it fall to the floor. She moved toward him and threw her arms around his neck. Her jeweled hair had fallen into a great loose mass, and valuable jewels rolled about the floor.

Emor's last night in the city was one of pleasure.

Chapter Eleven

That night as darkness fell on the Corillian village the inhabitants were happy and drank the wine of freedom. For the first time in ages the host of laughing, singing men, women, and children had their fill of fresh meat.

Whole Stayktons went onto the spits, and the crisp, savory smell of roasting meat perfumed the air. It was a great feasting for folk who had been denied such food for so long. They washed down the meat with wine, and their songs and laughter spiced the food.

It was a strange grouping: Orathians, Corillians, and the human known as Balzan of Endore whom they had made their leader. Balzan drank, laughed, and sang with them, Tarlene at his side, Taza and Jem before him, and surrounded by smiling faces whose names were lost but who formed a singular company of blood and races united now in their revolt against the Krells.

The night was for celebration. Pride and hope had been restored and there now was a comradeship of the oppressed. They held Balzan in awe. He was their leader and their god.

His name was mentioned many times around the fire. There was none among them, not even the children, who did not see Balzan as their champion.

Balzan sat among his friends and began to feel the wonderful inner glow of belonging. He once again possessed a family. He held Taza as his father image; Jem, his brother and comrade; Tarlene, his love, who he knew returned his affections with an ardor that bordered on worship.

They talked and weighed the things that had happened. Taza's eyes shone whenever he looked at Balzan.

"We can now enter the city. The strength of numbers

that we shall gather on our march will force Androth to listen to our demands."

Jem drank his wine lustily and took issue with the old Chronicler. "Demands? We will crush the Krells and give them a taste of the agony we have endured. I tell you this, if we can add to our numbers in force and with Balzan to lead us we will storm Manator and bring Androth to his knees."

But Balzan knew better. One victory in battle did not insure victory in the war. He lay with his head in Tarlene's lap, and she passed her fingers through his hair. Inside she was full of happiness and contentment. But a fire burned in Balzan. He looked at the twin moons in their glory and was filled with doubts. The weight of what lay ahead depressed him. He was committed to aid his friends and he knew that reprisals would be terrible. He had to lead the people who depended on him to the city of Manator itself—and destroy it.

The very thought, the enormity of thinking this made him sigh. Tarlene, seeing this, traced his lips with her fingers and her voice strayed into a song of her childhood days.

She sang, and his thoughts became pleasant, and he pushed the struggles that lay ahead from his mind temporarily.

"You must lead our people, Balzan," Jem exclaimed, "the world belongs to the Krells. We outnumber them tenfold, yet they remain the masters. Androth is the key; destroy him and the Krells are destroyed."

"He is only a man like we are, Jem," Balzan answered.

"No," Taza said. "He possesses powers of necromancy and evil that have made the Krells the feared warriors they are. Whatever transpires in the mountain of Zetar is the source of his strength. The machine speaks of Zetarians, but all we know is Androth. No one has defied his laws and lived."

Balzan did not answer but reflected inwardly. Taza was speaking the truth and his wisdom should not be ignored. The mountain of Zetar was reputed to be invulnerable to attack. Yet the youth was consumed with the desire to attempt it anyway. If the answers to the power of the Krells lay there, then he would go there to seek it out.

Tarlene stopped singing and asked him, "What are you

thinking, my love? Are you talking to the stars? Are they sharing secrets with you?" She half believed this. To her, Balzan was a god.

"There is nothing I would not share with you, Tarlene."

"Then what are your thoughts?"

"I was thinking that in your soft and warm arms I have found my love and my home."

"Then let us live, Balzan. Forget revolting against the Krells. We can leave and find a place of happiness. The world is large and we are in love."

"We can make our life here, Tarlene. If we band together who will stop us?"

"Androth" she said, and in the single word there was the power implicit, for Androth ruled the Krells, and the Krells had always been her masters.

"Then we will fight Androth," Balzan answered, "the people of your race and the Corillians will fight."

"No," she pleaded, "I want you to live."

He gently pulled her head down to his and kissed her. It was a night of contentment. Balzan lay there, among his friends, alongside the fire, and time stood still.

* * *

Before the brilliant colors of the cavernous room deep in the bowels of the mountain Androth brought the young alien's figure into his mind. Androth feared this youth who had begun to infiltrate and destroy his empire of conquest and vast riches.

The sleeping form of Balzan and the weaklings that gathered about him content with full bellies and wine-induced pleasure brought a hideous sneer to the face of the master of the Krells.

His Monitor, whom he had entrusted with the security of Manator, also brought rage to his decaying face. Even now, as he concentrated all of his dark powers on his visionary senses, he was still gripped with hate. He clearly saw his daughter Lenor languishing with his counsel Emor. When he returned to the city his first task would be in assigning Emor a new campaign. Like the Monitor, he was too ambitious.

Until the reversal process was complete he must remain in secrecy. But soon, with his powers of youth restored, the servants of his empire would pay for their laxness in dealing with the rebelling slaves.

Now he must summon his powers and risk more loss of strength to combat the alien Balzan. The threat he held to Androth made the sacrifice worth it.

Androth viewed the lifeless body before him with great concentration. Then he turned to the jeweled panel of the god Zetar and prostrated himself before the flashing lights. Whatever thought came to his mind, the god would materialize. With each materialization his strength ebbed.

But with the abundance of mine slaves the god would soon be satiated and Androth's youth would return in full bloom.

Androth pressed closer to the creature with humanoid head, lizard body, and folded bat wings. With a motion of his hand an intense blue light bathed the creature. The light coming from the panel gave a faint wailing sound.

As the light faded, Androth could see the creature's scaly legs and tail glistening with a blue sheen. Only one ingredient was lacking. The final substance that would animate the monster created by Androth's mind.

Androth drew a jeweled dagger from his sash and held it to the panel. An amber light engulfed it and it turned to the color of fire. He raised the dagger and plunged it into his wrist.

A drop of blood from his wrist fell on the creature. An emerald beam now pulsated from the panel and the single drop of blood spread and soon covered the entire body. The skin absorbed it completely in an instant.

The reaction was immediate.

The evil, hooded eyes flickered twice and then opened wide, gleaming yellow. It stretched its clawed feet and talons.

Slowly it swayed to a standing position. Although it towered over Androth it regarded its creator with fear. Androth smiled, as if he had finished a great work of art. He extended his bare arm to the creature as one would summon a pet. His arm showed the scar of the dagger above the wrist. The creature came forward, opened its bat wings, and bowed its hideous head to its master.

Now Androth rose, murmuring comfort into the ears of winged nightmare. He produced one of the hide tunics that the Endorians use as clothing. The creature clutched it,

99

then looked at its master, its tongue clicking in a staccato fashion, its head nodding in total subservience.

"Go and seek out the one who would destroy your father. Seek out the alien that bears the stench of the tunic you grasp. He is Balzan of Endore. Destroy him, bring me his blood digested in your body. Upon your return we will pour it with wine and you shall have everlasting life and a mate to follow you wherever you fly in the world of Androth."

The cavern ceiling opened at a gesture from the Krell and the creature flapped its wings violently and launched itself into the night.

Then Androth turned, his face even more heavily drawn than before. It approached the countenance of a skeleton with a wrinkled covering of decaying flesh. Still, he felt triumphant.

Guided by the magical power, the creature flew toward the Corillian village where Balzan slept.

It arrived in the Corillian village in the dead of night. Even with the multitude of sleeping humanity, the creature's senses singled Balzan out in an instant. Its long lizard tongue licked its humanoid lips and it waited. Hovering at a safe distance, it watched.

The firelight cast a glow upon the sleeping youth's features. The female cradled in his arms was sleeping contentedly.

The winged horror's yellow eyes focused on the exposed throat and the blood that would soon be consumed by the razor-sharp teeth that would rip the weak skin to shreds.

An eerie silence pervaded the atmosphere. The chilling winds of night penetrated old Taza's bones and required him to sit up and warm himself by the fire.

The creature hissed in anger as the sudden obstacle presented itself. The old one would die as well, for no power could halt the winged monster's mission.

Taza, in the grip of cold, reached for a wine jug and out of the corner of his eye noticed a movement from the trees.

"Balzan!" he yelled as the creature, its talons gleaming, swooped down on the sleeping youth.

Jem was on his feet in an instant from a dead sleep. At the creature's approach he flayed at it with his fist. Balzan, shocked out of a deep sleep, clambered to his feet, his sword in hand.

100

The creature collided with him and sent him sprawling. Jem, brandishing a flaming piece of wood, struck out at the attacking reptile. Its claws and talons scratched into his flesh. Balzan sliced at the wing and the monster turned, shrieking in agony. It lunged at Balzan, who fell on his back and caught the descending creature with his sword deep in its chest. With a hideous screech, the reptile dropped to the ground.

Inside the mountain of Zetar, Androth felt a sudden stabbing pain in his heart. He stopped in his tracks, his eyes bright. He staggered and sweat covered his body, cold and unrelenting. His face was a grotesque blend of rage and hysteria as he screamed into the echoing walls, "Bask in it, my young friend, for your life now is measured in hours."

The Krell master then dropped beside a pool of clear cold water and bathed his face.

His agony and pain were almost unbearable. A slow flicker of sudden inspiration played across his features.

Balzan was a worthy adversary. He could conquer the living and the creatures of Androth's invention, but what of the dead? They would be journeying to Manator and they must pass the burial temple of the Krell warriors.

Androth would reanimate the fallen dead of his glorious warriors and Balzan would be no more. Without him the herd he led would soon return to their purpose in life—serving the glory of the Krell empire.

Once again Androth turned to the pulsating lights of the panel that was the instrument of his awesome power.

Under Androth's resurrection the noble warriors who had served so well in life would once again serve in death.

"What was that?" Balzan exclaimed as he stood over the winged creature that stared at him with lifeless yellow eyes.

Jem kicked the lifeless form and snarled, "You can depend on Androth to send his little pets."

"Pets?" Balzan repeated.

"He has a menagerie of hellish beasts that none of us have ever seen before. It's almost as if he creates them himself. I know . . . that sounds like the utterings of a madman but Androth has powers that stagger the imagination."

"Well, whatever his powers are they're not invincible. The sword killed this thing as easily as it killed the meat we ate tonight."

Taza, concern written over his wrinkled face, spoke. "'The Chroniclers are assembling for the entrance to the city. We should leave now by darkness."

"I agree," Jem said. "I have many followers awaiting me and orders in the catacombs. The faster we reach the city, the better."

Balzan nodded in agreement. He glanced down at Tarlene and lifted her to her feet. "Do you feel up to it?"

"Yes," she answered.

"All right, let's move out now. By morning we should be close enough to the city for Taza and Jem to enter. I'll wait with Tarlene for your signal. Then I will lead the rest in support."

They moved out into the forest under the cover of darkness. Balzan did not know what destiny awaited him at the Krell city but whatever the consequences he was totally committed. He had an irresistible urge to beat the Krells into the dust, and an even stronger urge to pay a visit to the mountain where the Krell King awaited. It was going to take more than winged reptiles to save Androth when he felt Balzan's sword at his throat.

Chapter Twelve

The bulk of the force that Balzan led was left in conceal-ment in the caves that loomed on the fringe of the city of Manator. Tarlene begged to accompany Balzan, but he pre-vailed upon her to await his return. He followed Taza and Jem toward the Krell capital.

As the sun rose higher, the mists of the valley cleared and he looked at the valley below. The country was beauti-ful. The Krell city was gleaming in the distance like a jewel. The land was familiar to Taza and Jem. To Balzan it was an enchantment. Most of the slopes were tree-clad, but far below a river ran through the valley, and across the river there was a darkening which was a huge bridge. The square cultivated fields showed evidence of the Krell prosperity.

They had topped the summit of the hill, and Jem looked down into the valley, alert for any sign of ambush; his sense of being watched, pursued, had grown to be an obses-sion by now.

This would be a good place for an ambush, as they came up over the hill.

But the road and valley lay bare before them in the cloudy sunlight, and Jem frowned, trying to relax his tense muscles by an act of will. Balzan sensed his young compan-ion's uneasiness and the older man's weariness.

"Let's rest here awhile," he said, "there's plenty of time and Taza looks like he's about to drop."

The old man nodded and slumped to the ground, exhal-ing. Jem scanned the terrain and nodded. "It seems quiet. I doubt if they are searching this close to the city. I feel pity for my friends in Orathia, though. By this time, Androth's number one butcher has probably leveled the entire prov-ince."

"Who is that?" Balzan asked.

"Fleet Counsel Emor, a devil. I fear his sword and determination more than Androth's little pets. He's a warrior and he is no fool."

"If he's in Orathia then that will be in our favor. The less Krells the better," Taza offered.

"His airships are swift. It won't take long to recall him. That is why we must act with surprise. It is in our favor to strike swiftly and then wait to snare the Lord Counsel when he returns from killing old men and women," Jem sneered.

Refreshed from their period of rest, the trio proceeded on toward Manator. They came to a clearing of emerald green where a multitude of monoliths was neatly and geometrically placed.

"What is this?" Balzan queried.

"The burial grounds of the Krell warriors," Taza answered.

Balzan stopped for a moment to study the curious crystalline structures; the cemetery was completely foreign to him, since the Endorians were cremated upon death. He had never before experienced a tradition where bodies were placed into the ground and their memory displayed by stones above them.

Taza and Jem had continued ahead and Balzan, enthralled at this latest discovery of Krell culture, had totally forgotten their presence.

A scream ripped the air, shattering the calm. It was a painful sound, a hoarse fearful scream, a scream that could come only from dying lips.

Balzan stared in amazement as he watched the old Chronicler slide slowly to the ground, limp and unmistakably dead; his throat was a single long gash from which blood spouted like a crimson fountain.

Balzan drew his sword and rushed to his fallen comrade. Jem also, with sword in hand, was turning in every direction looking for the unseen assailant.

Taza lay staring at nothing—the pumping blood slowly obliterating his features. An invisible claw of steel had ripped out the throat of what seconds before had been a living breathing man.

"Look," Jem croaked, clutching the hilt of his blade. He pointed to the rise before them. Balzan turned to see several shadowy forms, strange and hardly humanoid. The light brought them into focus and Balzan saw by the deterioration of their tunics and the absence of flesh on parts of their bodies that they were in actuality reanimated corpses.

Balzan and Jem backed slowly to get the sun from their eyes. Fury pulsed in Balzan's blood, but an icy wave of reason told him coldly to await their first lunge. His brain needed time to assimilate the horrors before him.

The walking dead men paused and Balzan became aware of the grim quiet that lay over the burial yard. Suddenly there were splotches of blood on the stones. A strange disquiet, a sickening unease. He knew that something beyond reason was creeping over him. He fought it off with all his fiber and being.

He turned to see Jem standing as if in a trance—his mouth gaping, his eyes staring in dumb horror.

Balzan grasped him, and the sound of his voice brought him back to reality. "What are these things?"

The Orathian could only manage an idiotic sound. He began laughing hysterically and dropped his sword.

Balzan grabbed him. "Pick up your sword, damn you," he rasped.

Instead Jem placed his hands over his head and lay down in a fetal position, half sobbing, half laughing.

Now in the grip of angry frustration, Balzan bellowed at the creatures that covered him in a half circle.

"Come on! Let's see what rot and bones can do against a man of flesh and blood."

Balzan's voice was hard; he kept it that way with a fierce effort. "Come on!"

Balzan met the dead hollow stares with a level blue gaze.

One of the misshapen corpses staggered toward Balzan. In its decayed hand it clutched the rusted metal sword it had been buried with.

Balzan parried the blow easily and plunged his sword to the hilt in the corpse's chest. The corpse stared for an instant. The wound made by the blade was visible but not bloody—only a few drops of a gluey fluid oozed from it and immediately coagulated.

The others began moving toward Balzan in slow lumbering half-steps. What was more terrible than the loathesome look of the dead men was the sudden realization that they also were pawns of Androth's necromancy. Mindless dead tissue animated by a force that was beyond human understanding.

· Balzan slashed at the head of the closest creature. It staggered slightly, then moved slowly toward him.

Above Balzan, dark clouds had formed as though some baleful force of consciousness sensed the need for a macabre setting.

Balzan's next blow half severed the head. He waited for it to fall. It did not. Only a trace of torment at this unnatural resurrection could be seen in the obscene contours of the corpse's features.

The second of the three corpses now lunged awkwardly at Balzan. The youth's sword plunged into its neck below the jaw. The corpse ignored the gaping wound in its charnel flesh and swung with its decrepit sword. Balzan sliced at its legs and brought the undead creature to its knees. The third rushed him. Now, in sudden close proximity with the terrible undead, Balzan shrank away in dread—not so much in fear as from physical disgust. It was the same revulsion that would come from any putrefying smell. The creature's inaccurate wielding of the sword presented a pathetic picture of despair. There was no anger in the face; the fathomless eyes were vacant.

Balzan's next savage swipe tore the rotten tunic away and exposed a mesh of gray rotted intestines.

The brain, nourished by unnatural sources, stopped to look at the wound Balzan had inflicted.

Balzan, utilizing both hands and wielding the blade like a club, severed the head. The corpse fell and lay silent. The remaining corpse moved at Balzan, slashing to and fro with his blade.

A flash of lightning illuminated his face and he stopped and peered up at the slashing rain. It was as though illusion were mixing with reality.

A bolt of lightning split the sky and plunged earthward. It seized upon the rusted sword and reduced it to molten metal.

Instantly, the corpse was engulfed in flames. There were no sounds of pain or terror as the burning flesh was engulfed in white heat.

The wretch pitched downward and lay burning as the sky opened and Balzan was drenched with the cooling rain.

It was a long time before he remembered Jem and revived him. Androth's spell had worked on him and had turned him into a mass of hysteria, but it had failed on Balzan.

Recovered now, Jem could remember nothing.

Balzan let it stay that way. He would vent his anger on the one responsible. . . .

Androth.

* * *

The evening meal in the elaborate salon of Manator's illustrious Monitor was festive. On the part of the Monitor, it was less than ingrained conceit that he held himself above his guests for the evening. The citizens who dined tonight were a rich class that made their fortunes out of wars and the mines.

The Monitor could not enjoy a meal in a prone position on a couch, it impaired his digestion; so he and his guests dined at an immense table. He presented them with game and fowl, with fine fruits from the Morgana provinces, and snow-chilled wine brought from the pinnacles by riders on swift mounts.

There was music, good food, and dancing girls. His guests reflected his tastes. They reclined in their chairs sipping wine and discussing the latest developments of the empire.

The evening was not a total success, however, since the special invitation to dine had been completely ignored by Princess Lenor. It was obvious that she was displeased with him for sending her lover, Emor, from the city. The Monitor knew only too well that her displeasure would be related to her father when he returned. If by chance Androth failed to return to Manator from his retreat, his daughter would have to be the victim of a tragic accident.

The sly Monitor knew that once Lenor was upon the throne, his life would be taken in short order. Thus, he had arranged, if the ultimate came to pass, that he would be the first to strike.

He dismissed Lenor from his mind and returned to the pleasantries of his dinner guests' light conversation. Tomorrow the first reprisal against the rebelling provinces would be delivered with a shattering blow. Although he despised the vain and egotistic Emor, he respected the qualities of leadership and total dedication he possessed in the systematic elimination of all who defied Krell rule. As a mercenary, Emor had no peers, with the possible exception of himself, the Monitor thought with a smile.

* * *

Beneath the city, shielded from the pounding rain, the catacombs were somber and angry. Jem mourned the loss of Taza, and Balzan sat moodily in the distance as the assembled Orathians and Corillians awaited the next order. Arc, Jem's comrade, brought the youth a mug of wine and introduced himself.

"You are an honored ally, Balzan. I, a Corillian, embrace you in friendship."

"Thank you, Arc. I also."

Jem joined the men and spoke gravely. "The Monitor has canceled the tribute. Any unlawful assembly will be dealt with severely."

Balzan chewed on his lip a moment before answering. "All right, then we'll use another method for bargaining. Understand me, Jem, I am not going to kill Krells indiscriminately, but I am going to see that Androth pays!"

"What is your plan?"

"I want four good men besides you—armed men. And then I want you to lead me back to the dungeon the same way you took me out."

"What for?" Jem exclaimed.

"I'm going to pay a little visit to Androth's daughter."

"The Princess Lenor? You're mad. You can never reach her quarters."

Balzan smiled. "We'll soon see, won't we?"

Jem leaned back against the rock and stared at the youth in a combination of wonder and mirth.

"If it's the dungeon you want, my friend, then it will be the dungeon you get. I would follow you into hell."

"There's a possibility that may be just where we're headed."

Chapter Thirteen

The grim iron fortress lay beneath the palace along the sea. It stood apart from the maze of narrow streets and crowded structures. As the small band made their way through the catacombs to the secret entrance their eyes remained keen and their senses alert.

Jem led them through a tangle of twisted corridors to an ancient doorway that was so old and forgotten that it did not appear on the maps of the city.

Its original purpose had been long forgotten, and no one, save men that were forced to rendezvous and plot in the catacombs, knew of its presence.

No keyhole showed in the massive, slime-encrusted lock, but Jem deftly pressed a knob that was invisible to the casual eye. The door silently opened inward and they entered solid blackness. Above them was a bare cylindrical shaft of massive stone.

Reaching into the corner with the sureness of familiarity, Jem found the slab of stone that composed the door. He lifted it quickly and Balzan and the other men followed him down into the aperture beneath.

Stone steps led downward into a narrow tunnel that ran straight toward the foundations that snaked to the upper levels of the dungeon.

The men moved silently from the darkness up three levels to an iron door that opened into a corridor. The dank interior was forbidding; rats scurried at regular intervals beneath their feet. The massive stone walls were wet and mossy. The floor was deep-worn by generations of staggering feet, the ceiling was gloomy in the dim light cast by the torches set in niches.

A figure emerged from the far end of the corridor. The men darted into the shadows and watched.

"One of the jailers," Jem whispered to Balzan.

The Krell who trudged down the grim corridor was powerfully built. From his shoulders hung a long coil of black whip; he carried a caron in his hand. As he went down the corridor, another figure came hobbling up it, a bent old man, stooping under the weight of the water pail and lantern he bore.

"These dogs are watered," he grumbled. "I am going to bed. I leave them to your tender care."

"Consider yourself fortunate, old man, that you are able to sleep. These vermin must die to get rest," the guard answered.

"Yes, Master, yours is the sweeter of the duties—for you can at least depart at your leisure, while I am as good as a prisoner."

"You should have paid your taxes, old fool. At least you are not in the mines. Now be off, I must continue my rounds."

The old water-bearer limped on down the corridor, still grumbling, and the guard resumed his rounds. A few strides carried him around a turn in the corridor, and he absently noted that a door was slightly open at his left. He passed it before he realized his mistake, and then it was too late.

A cat-like step and rustle warned him, but before he could turn a heavy arm hooked about his throat from behind, crushing the cry before it could reach his lips. In his surge of panic he knew he had met his death. Jem's blade slashed his throat silently and accurately.

In the jailers' section, lit only by a guttering torch, two Krells were occupied with gambling at a crude table. One voiced a low involuntary cry at the sight of the six grim men framing the doorway.

One Krell leaped toward his sword, the other darted for the stairs. Jem's dagger, accurately thrown, plunged into his back. The other Krell lunged at Balzan, who parried the blow and then crushed the Krell's breast with a vicious counterstroke. The next blow from Balzan's weapon caved in his skull.

Balzan went to the Krells' storage chest and retrieved his therb and precious Kharnite sword. Jem peered up the dimly lit steps. There was no sign of any alarm from the upper levels. He signaled the others, and they turned off into a side passage and quickly emerged into another, broader corridor which ran parallel to the one they had just deserted.

They followed this one only a few yards, then went to another passage. Spiraling upward was the private staircase that led to the palace. The men climbed the stairs and emerged into a marble-floored corridor in the west wing of the palace.

After the dimness of the dungeon and staircase, the broad lighted chamber strained their eyes.

At the end of the corridor, two Krell guards stood at the entrance of the Princess Lenor's private apartments.

Balzan whispered a few quick words to Jem, who nodded. Then they sprang forward, their blades flickering with the speed of striking snakes.

The two guards sank to the floor bathed in blood from the sudden furious onslaught.

Balzan told Jem and the others to stand guard hidden outside Lenor's door. He entered the chambers of the Krell princess.

She looked up from a pile of cushions. She was dressed in a sumptuous gown. Her two handmaidens cringed, but the Krell princess regarded the youth with a cool stare. She waved her hand and the maids departed like frightened children.

"Would you like more wine?"

"Not likely," Balzan answered.

She laughed aloud delightfully and quite artificially. "Yes, I seem to remember the last wine I offered you did not agree with you."

"I'm flattered that you even remember me, Princess," Balzan said with mock humility.

"When I summon my guards to remove your head, I will have it mounted so that I can always remember you."

"Don't bother, Princess, your guards are dead and my men are waiting outside your chambers."

Then, leaning forward a little, she said in a voice that snickered like a sword in the ribs: "You really think that you will ever leave this palace alive?"

"With you as my shield I have a chance. Or do you think your guards might not recognize you?"

She raised her eyebrows in a look of pure hatred. "You

111

dare threaten the daughter of Androth, you filth? I would die before I let you place your hand upon me."

"That may very well be your fate then, Princess," Balzan said coldly and without hesitation.

"You came here to take me prisoner?" she asked incredulously.

"I have come to escort you to be with your subjects, Princess, and then perhaps your father will listen to the people he has enslaved. Otherwise there will be war."

"War?" She laughed. "With whom? Staykton herders and mine rats?" She allowed her hatred to spew forth. "And you? A creature that smells of the sewers! My father will crush you like a dried leaf."

"Fine. I accept the challenge," he said, watching her every move.

She advanced toward him, apparently without apprehension. "You are not an Orathian. Why have you interfered with the Krell order?"

"It was the Krells that interfered with me. I offered friendship and instead I was offered death."

She moved closer. Balzan saw two tiny needles extend from the ring on her finger.

Seeing that he had noticed her deadly ring she halted. Then, her eyes flaring wide, she lunged suddenly.

With a movement too swift for the eye to follow, Balzan's hand grasped her wrist. "Not this time, Princess."

Her smooth almond skin was as cold as marble, yet still there was no fear in the wide dark eyes which regarded him.

"Very well, I will remove it," she volunteered.

He released her wrist and she removed the jeweled ring and tossed it to the floor.

"Don't be a fool, Balzan, I can offer you more wealth than you have ever dreamed of, and I can offer you other pleasures as well."

"I'm sure you could, Princess."

"You are young, handsome. Why not join us instead of resisting us? The joys of Manator are the greatest in the world. Everything you could possibly want is here."

"What I want is not here," he said coldly. "What your people offer is a fate that I would rather die than accept."

"You are a strange man, Balzan," she purred. She

112

crossed the room and turned to him. "But, nevertheless, you are a man, aren't you?"

Stretching herself on a couch with feline suppleness, she intertwined her fingers behind her sleek head and regarded him from under her long lashes. "If you want me as a prisoner, you will have to take me in those strong arms and carry me."

"No, I could kill you," he said pleasantly, "that's a lot easier than carrying you."

She laughed, shook her burnished locks, and spread her arms sensuously.

Balzan ignored her erotic gesture. "I haven't the time for your amusement. Now get to your feet or I will drag you."

Rising lithely she came to him, rose on tiptoe, and flung her arms about his neck. Frowning down into her beautiful upturned countenance, he was aware of a fearful fascination and an overpowering lust for her.

"Tell me you don't want me," she whispered. She threw her head back, closed her eyes, and parted her lips. With a curse he tore her away and flung her, sprawling, across the couch.

She reared up on the couch like a serpent poised to strike, all the fires of hell blazing in her wide eyes. Her lips drew back. "You'll never leave this room alive, you fool."

She then bolted to the terrace with Balzan in pursuit. As she raced outside she screamed for the guards. As Balzan reached to pull her inside, she struggled and her silver gown ripped in Balzan's fingers as she fell backward over the terrace. Her scream cut through Balzan like a knife. Then he saw her twisted and broken body sprawled in the courtyard below.

Through his physical revulsion ran a sense of a shattered dream of his manhood. A wave of futility swept over him. He felt a dim fear of all men's dreams of strength and honor. He had caused the death of a woman and he cursed aloud.

Whatever hope may have existed for a peaceful solution now was as shattered as the lovely body below him.

Sounds from the corridor told him the palace was aroused. He drew his sword and rejoined Jem and the others in the corridor.

Outside, his comrades were locked in combat with the Krells.

Balzan caught the closest one to him. The Krell fell backward, his face a smear of blood and bone.

Then Balzan whirled into the nearest group of guards on the other side of Jem. Using the Kharnite sword, he cut through them like grain.

The men fought brilliantly, all fired with vitality. Balzan fought in a frenzy. A quick slash sent a Krell tumbling backward with his entrails spilling out. Balzan stabbed, thrust, and sliced. Two of his comrades fell but, when the last guard fell, over a dozen Krells had died.

They broke for the passageway but it was blocked by advancing Krells. Jem slashed into them, swinging his sword like an axe. Three of the Orathians were trapped behind Balzan by another group and the fourth was killed by a Krell blow to the back.

Balzan saw, at the far end of the corridor, another door open and a mass of Krells swarmed through it brandishing swords.

He sheathed his sword and lifted a table over his head and hurled it at the stained glass of the window. The glass shattered into thousands of colored shards.

Balzan yelled to Jem. The two men sprang through the window in headlong dives toward the sea a hundred feet below.

* * *

They came ashore breathing in deep gasps. The sand and solid earth brought a solace to them that was beyond description. They had fought the waves for over an hour and exhaustion closed over them like a blanket of blackness.

* * *

When Balzan awoke, the sun was high in the sky. White puffs of clouds danced above him in a brilliant sky. Jem lay sprawled beside him, snoring in contentment. After awakening him with a good-humored kick, the men moved out along the shoreline back to the caves where their band of followers waited.

As they moved from the beach into the forest, Balzan saw in the distance great stone faces carved on the rocks of a mountain.

"What is that?" he asked Jem.

"The mountain of Zetar."

"The mountain that Androth retreats to?"

"Yes."

"I want to see that place," he said with a gleam in his eyes.

"No. Balzan, there is no way to enter it. Androth has it guarded by a carnivore, it's completely impenetrable."

"Nothing is impenetrable, Jem."

"That mountain is, believe me."

Balzan's deliberations were halted abruptly by something that caught his gaze. Perhaps it was a trick of the sun, but it looked like a shadow of something withered and bent, like an elderly man or woman.

One of its hands was pointing to the mountain. Then, before his eyes, the shadow faded away.

"Return to the caves. I'll join you later. I'm going to the mountain."

"Balzan," Jem entreated.

The youth turned and smiled, "I'll be all right. Go along now."

He plunged immediately into the undergrowth.

Balzan made his way through the forest. Twice he lost his way. But on both occasions he thought he saw an old hooded figure in the distance who beckoned him onward, and it was in that direction he followed.

He reached the temple at the base of the mountain. Two pillars supported the entrance and massive stone faces lined the rock like sentries. Balzan saw the hooded figure disappear within the entrance. As he approached, a voice rasped from within.

"Beware of the Crixma."

The hooded figure disappeared, smiling, for he and he alone knew the only passageway that would avoid the beast.

Inside the mountain the eerie atmosphere pressed down upon him with an almost physical force. Balzan shrugged off the depressing influence and gripped the hilt of the Kharnite sword firmly.

He moved cautiously through the passage, his eyes slowly becoming accustomed to the gloom. Then he halted.

He stood completely still, ears sharpened to the utmost, nostrils widened to catch the faintest scent. He heard a low guttural growl deep within the passageway.

He advanced cautiously.

The path made a sudden turn a hundred paces farther on. At the corner, his sharp eyes sought the cause of the sound he had heard.

Then a hoarse bellow reached his ears. He peered into the darkness.

With a growl, a giant spider with a hideous anthropoid head reared from its hiding place with bared and dripping fangs. At that instant the sword in Balzan's hand flashed.

The spider-ape measured over fifty feet and moved on long bowed legs that were armed with sharp curved claws. Its jaws were gigantic, set with saber teeth. The swellings at the sides of its head pulsated with a crimson beat. Its breath stank of moldering corpses.

It paused for a moment as if savoring the anticipation of its dinner.

More quickly than he expected, the giant beast attacked. Balzan rolled beneath the stilted legs and chopped at the belly. Balzan lunged and rammed the sword between the muscles of the side, then into the soft internal tissues.

With a side lunge of its head, it hurled Balzan into the wall twenty feet away.

Balzan sliced into the lower part of the lumbering giant's jaw and it uttered a shriek of pain. His arm ached, but he forced his body to continue its assault.

Grimly, he put his whole strength into a desperate lunge at the underbelly. The blade went in like a knife through butter. The beast writhed in agony. Balzan struck again and the beast shrieked louder. Next Balzan concentrated on the pulsating red spots on its head. His next blow shattered the right one and the creature stumbled onto its rear legs.

Balzan then rammed the blade between the gaping jaws and darkness of its gullet. The blade was snatched from his grasp by the last convulsions of the dying beast. Again he was tossed against the wall. With a final tremor, the beast collapsed; blood flowed from it, covering the entire floor. Balzan retrieved his sword and continued along the passageway.

Suddenly, directly ahead, there was an immense stone stairway.

Chapter Fourteen

At the foot of the steps was a cavernous bell-shaped room with cold rock walls. There were stalagmites and stalactites in profusion on the roof and floor. A tiny pinpoint of light shown down from the center of the roof; the sun entered between the stone faces that topped the outer mound.

This light shone on the figure seated upon a circular stone dais decorated with strange twisted symbols. Nearby a lighted brazier threw a flickering light on Balzan's face.

The figure rose shakily, betraying great age, and, stepping down from the dais, reached out a gnarled hand to the youth. Balzan, in innocence, mistook it for a gesture of friendship.

Suddenly the youth was hurled backward as a whirlwind field of force engulfed him. He was on his feet in an instant, his sword unsheathed and ready. He advanced toward the old figure again.

Balzan shielded his eyes as flames burst toward him like a concentrated tornado of energy, twisting and growing. Out of it, the figure's voice boomed at him in a sonorous voice.

"Balzan of Endore, you have defeated the Crixma by your cunning and strength, but now you will face the instrument of your death."

Balzan watched as the old man stepped into the flames. His presence fused into a brilliant white light that was impossible to look at. With a rush of wind, the shimmering force field engulfed Balzan. The old man reappeared and his shrill laugh deafened Balzan by its thunderous crescendo. Now for the first time Balzan saw the face. It was skeletal and had the mummified look of centuries of death. Bal-

117

zan gazed upon a countenance composed of decayed and gray flesh, burning yellow eyes, and a mocking smile.

"Come, Balzan. Come with your sword that I can turn to dust with a breath from my nostril."

Balzan snarled and rushed the figure standing in the fire. As he raised his sword to strike the mocking figure he lunged at became his adopted father, Lomar. The old Endorian's face was twisted in a grimace of agony. His fur and flesh were bleeding profusely.

Balzan stared incredulously at the figure before him. The old man raised a four-fingered hand in a pleading gesture. The old Cat Man's olive slits bored into Balzan. Balzan could not strike. As he stood immobilized, a shock wave rent the air. Smoke and dust poured into the cavern. Large chunks of rock bagan to drop from the roof.

Sections of pillar came rolling down the stone steps. One piece missed Balzan by inches. Then, in horror, he saw the figure of Lomar scream as a thick stalactite crashed down upon him. The laughter came again and built to a hideous wail.

"What now, Balzan? Do you feel the fury of Androth?"

"I feel the fury of an old man that has resorted to a magician's tricks. Come and face me, Androth, if you dare."

The laughter resumed. "Magician's tricks," the voice roared. "I'll show you magician's tricks!"

Balzan saw the old figure that was Androth standing now in a passageway. Androth turned and disappeared into it. Balzan followed him. The passageway was lit by torches that burned with an odd green light. The walls were lined with carved statues, the faces the same as the giant ones that lay at the entrance.

Balzan followed the twisting narrow passage until it opened into another mammoth room. Vast pillars held up an overhanging cliff which had been carved into an ornate ceiling.

On an altar stood another huge statue of the god Zetar. The statue had been mounted at the top of a flight of stairs and, behind it, a great circle of precious gems sparkled like fire.

Androth stood before the shrine, prostrated himself before the steps, and spoke softly. Balzan could not hear the words, but when the figure stood he appeared to have lost some of his wrinkles and the lines of age around his eyes.

He spoke to Balzan in an ugly unfamiliar tongue. Then he pointed at the statue. With a creak and a wail of tortured metal, the statue and its foundation opened to reveal a passageway behind it. Androth turned to Balzan.

"Now, Balzan of Endore, behold a substance of purity and evil magnified to blend into your heart and mind like burning metal. Its sight will drain your strength, blood, and courage. Behold!"

For a moment there was nothing but silence. The flickering of the torches was the only sound in the immense room.

Then it emerged from the darkness—a writhing mass of interwined, hissing, snakelike bodies with vaguely humanoid faces and atrophied arms.

Balzan moved to the center of the room to meet the hellish creature that seemed to him, in a curious way, not a flesh and blood figure but something fabricated in the dark world of sorcery.

The thing paused at the top step, swaying slightly. Then its six heads all fastened on Balzan and it approached him slowly.

But Balzan was already circling the lumbering creature for the opening gambit of the duel. The weird faces all seemed familiar to him, yet they were as alien as was the creature.

A smile seemed to flicker over the lips of each head and, while Balzan watched grimly, each of the arms extended razor-sharp talons.

Never had Balzan faced such a confusing creature. Under Androth's influence the creature seemed to possess six independent minds. As its mass drew closer Balzan struck out and neatly sliced off one of the grinning heads in one swipe. Instantly the head collapsed like a punctured balloon. Semi-fluid gray matter spurted from it. The protruding eyes merely stared, the muscle of the mouth opened and closed. Then, where the severed head had been connected to the writhing bodies, another head took its place.

Balzan watched all this in wonder; it was as if he were dueling with a shadow. Engrossed with the heads, Balzan was unaware that one of the talons circled his leg. The thing pulled and the impact hurled Balzan to the ground. Then as the arms closed to seize him, he drove the sharp blade deep into the mass of flesh. The hissing sound intensified and then Balzan slashed the talon from his leg. He sprang to his feet and saw that the loathesome arm he had severed had rolled from the body and was now crawling behind him on short spider-like legs. Immediately the arm gave evidence of intelligent animation as it lunged for Balzan's throat. He parried it and sent it flying toward the altar. In the space of time it took Balzan to turn, six arms were reaching for him. He slashed and parried. As severed heads flew, new ones took their place, while the discarded ones circled for rear attacks.

It was a series of thrusts and lunges, but Balzan was not gaining, he was tiring—fast. The creature seemed totally lacking in rage or emotion or the capacity to express either. Its protruding eyes simply stared and occasionally the muscles of its mouths opened and closed. But by far the most gruesome sight were the heads crawling about biting at his legs.

Balzan attacked even the flailing tendons with precision and skill. One tendon smashed against his forehead, driving him into the wall. As Balzan's dazed brain cleared he lunged in reflex as the combined assault of the six heads charged. His sword accurately chopped and severed, but to no avail. As rapidly as Balzan would sever one of the hideous heads another would take its place.

Balzan, in desperation, raced up the steps of the shrine to evade the creature. When he turned, the blinding white flash came again and the creature vanished. In its place appeared the figure of Androth, more youthful and still laughing hideously. Balzan bared his teeth and lunged down the steps to the Krell.

He plunged into a mass of sinking earth. Startled by this unexpected sensation, as up to now the floor of the cave had been solid rock, Balzan was aware that he was groping helplessly in the ooze. Dripping water echoed from every direction. Androth, with a wave of his hand, transformed the cave in an instant. Looking down, Balzan discovered he was now treading on dried skulls.

The wail of Androth's high-pitched voice caused him to turn to the shrine again.

"In a moment, Balzan of Endore, the things you encounter will be real, not creatures of your imagination. Soon I will be strong again and I shall slay you as I would slay a dog."

"Unless I slay you first, ruler of slaves," Balzan rasped.

Androth raised his arm again and the white brilliance engulfed Balzan. A low-pitched wail began echoing from all sides, then built in intensity. The youth dropped his sword and placed his hands to his ears. The whine grew louder as Balzan's eardrums seemed to be shattering.

Androth turned to the jeweled panel in the shrine. He placed his hands upon the panel and the jewels glowed faintly at first and then burst into a brilliance of dazzling light. The high-pitched wail ceased and Balzan fell to the ground.

Now the entire cave was aflame with brilliant lights that sparkled and turned the stalagmites and stalactites into a burst of scarlet, emerald, and gold.

Androth, his hands shaking, fell prostrate before the lights. When he rose he was a young man again.

Balzan stood transfixed by the miraculous transformation of the Krell ruler.

Androth turned to Balzan. "Now, the energy of youth is mine once more, and with it the invulnerability of Zetar."

Balzan's young face darkened. "Then let us duel, Krell. I tire of your games."

Androth raised his arms in supplication to the god Zetar and his voice rang out in the vast cavern in a fearsome impassioned plea. "Great Zetar, I, who have given you thousands of sacrifices from the mines, now give you the ultimate sacrifice—the human who comes from a world that challenges the might of Zetar. With his blood upon your altar, the Feast of Zetar will be purified for a millennium. I give you his blood for the gift you have bestowed on me."

After the outburst, silence. Androth was staring, straining his eyes into the brilliant lights.

Balzan grabbed his blood-stained sword and prepared to meet the Krell king.

Androth laughed harshly and drew his sword. The two men circled around each other. Androth wore the smile of a supremely confident victor, for the power of Zetar was within him.

At the first clash of their swords, Balzan realized what he was up against. For, as the noise echoed round the vast cavern, the power of Androth's blade sent Balzan to his knees as he parried the first blow.

121

"You are weak, alien," said Androth tauntingly. "Perhaps if you beg I will be merciful."

The lunge and parry of the fight continued with Androth sending Balzan back with each thrust.

"You seem weary, alien."

"Do I?" Balzan said, trying to disguise the helplessness he was beginning to feel, and he slashed back fiercely. Androth's evil laughter filled the air.

Balzan, bewildered, fought on. But he was barely stopping Androth's savage blows. It was hopeless. Then Androth, overconfident, angled his sword too high.

Their swords clashed. With an expert flick, Balzan sent his opponent's weapon flying through the air. The flying projectile smashed into the jeweled panel, an explosion roared, and flames shot into the air.

Androth stood frozen. Suddenly he moved to his left and his outstretched arms flailed at the panel.

Balzan heard Androth's gasps for breath as he plowed toward the now-dimming lights of the panel.

Balzan saw the Krell stagger and fall at its base. Androth turned and glared at Balzan. He had aged in an instant. His weak frail body seemed several sizes too small for his tunic. White hair sprouted wispily where black had been a moment before.

Most shocking was his face.

It was not that it was incredibly old—Balzan could accept that. It was the deep depravity that made the most impression. It was his red-rimmed, yellow eyes and the twisted embittered mouth.

Androth struggled to his feet. "Well, Balzan, you have triumphed. Now, if there is mercy in your heart, end it now."

The youth approached the figure who could barely stand.

"You have succeeded in doing what centuries of warfare could not accomplish. You have destroyed the light that brought eternal life."

The Krell's words rang in Balzan's brain. "Was it life, Androth? Or was it in reality your own form of slavery?"

Androth lifted Balzan's sword and placed the end of it against his own breast. "You are weak, alien."

Then Androth grasped the blade with both hands and pulled it to him. The sword entered his heart. As Androth tensed, impaled on the steel, Balzan drew back. Androth turned and, with a last great cry, fell at the foot of the god Zetar.

Balzan walked to the steps and dropped down upon them. The withered body of the Krell king lay dead. The light that powered an entire city was now but a rose-colored dimness.

Then Balzan saw a flash of light from behind the panel. He followed its rays.

Under normal conditions such a brain wave might have been alarming, but not now, for suddenly Balzan let a grin come to his face. He raced to the panel. Behind it was a chamber below a natural wall of rock. The excitement within him urged him on. The chamber led directly into another immeasurably larger cavern. Rounding a stack of rocks, Balzan was stunned by the vastness and breathtaking grandeur of the scene.

Two large beams set high on the cavern walls brought in streams of intense light which illuminated a great circular section of giant stones. Each of these carved monoliths stood as sentries around the most magnificent console Balzan had ever seen.

And the lights . . . the colors. Millions of flashing dancing colors reflected on the timeless walls. It was as if the sun had been funneled into the room and exploded into a myriad of spectacular fragments.

Balzan had to shield his eyes from the brilliance. The god Zetar was a—computer.

Yet, this computer was different, not metallic and cold, but bathed in an aura of life itself, life that generated the magnificent lights. Balzan felt strangely small in its awesome presence. He could easily understand how Androth had accepted this computer from some vast intelligence as a god.

Balzan was racked with a sudden sense of foreboding and fear that seemed to clutch at his vital organs. A shadowy substance loomed before him. It flickered in and out of reason; whatever power lurked behind the dark edge of shadow that clouded his mind, it was immense.

Stark terror and despair clawed at him for a moment, so painfully that he half wondered if he had been wounded. Then, with a deep breath, he realized what he had to do, and focused on the power source before him.

He raised his blade and stood confronting the great menace. Dark mist swirled before his eyes. Somewhere in the dark of his mind he heard a whisper that was a blend of every tongue that he had ever heard. Balzan wondered if he were going mad. The lights faded in brilliance and the room was colored by a pleasant glow that seemed to pulsate with each beat of Balzan's heart. Swirling shadows engulfed him, their green glows changing behind a wall of mist to amber, then to a red glow, like distant burning coals, and again the mist blotted them out. He became aware that he was shaking all over. His mind could not be clouded by lights, colors. Whatever power it possessed was not human, but an intelligence programmed by a life form.

Balzan reacted to the bewilderment of his spirit in anger. He hurled his sword into the center of the console. The blade vaporized in midair. Then a black arrow of force was hurled at him and he was engulfed in a spinning momentum of gray form and matter without substance. He tried to clear his brain, but the grayness remained. Finally he permitted his body to sink to the ground. The fleeting grayness darted across his eyes until it merged into blackness.

* * *

The sound of his name recalled Balzan from a blind world of nothingness and distorted memory to full alertness. Balzan passed a sweating palm over his forehead. He sat up, shaking his head, sweating and trembling with the memory of—what? He was totally disoriented. He looked around, searching for something familiar—a human face, any sign of life. He felt as if his mind had been erased, as if he were a fetus gasping in some horrible womb of pulsating lights. He felt detached from his body, as if he were watching himself in a grim struggle for reason. He reeled as he appeared to have intensified all of his senses. He smelled the great stench of burning cat fur. He was thinking of Lomar again. But why? Other thoughts pushed now at his brain; it was as if it had been borrowed and was being returned memory by memory.

Balzan then reeled with the horrid shock. The computer had picked his mind and had completely digested every bit of knowledge that he possessed in its memory banks.

He riveted his eyes on the giant console that could blast

him lifeless with a single scorching breath. He rose to his feet and stared at the brilliant lights.

How could he combat something that was so totally perfect?

Balzan stepped toward it, warily, and waited. . . .

Chapter Fifteen

Balzan lowered his eyes to the flashing luminescence of blue. Deep inside the wall small ribbons and worms of color moved, slowly, like a beating heart. Zetar's heart.

His senses were sharpened to the utmost. The ghastly things he had encountered thrust themselves on his consciousness like attacking demons. But with iron self-possession, he shrugged off his fears and waited.

Then a noise like a thunderclap rang with booming crashes between the echoing walls, and a shrill wailing cry made Balzan's blood run cold. With a swish of wings, an unearthly being swooped from the upper darkness. Like a vision from hell it plummeted down at Balzan.

The young human flung himself aside barely in time to avoid the razor-sharp claws of the creature. Then his sword swept in a glittering arc. The winged horror flopped away, howling. One arm, severed at the elbow, gushed foul-smelling blood.

It was the same creature that had attacked Jem and him —the creature of Androth's magic. The thing lived even though its master was dead.

With a scream it sprang toward the youth again. The monster spread its wings to soar as it sprang. At the last moment, Balzan evaded the claws of the remaining hand and put all his strength into a ripping thrust.

The sword tore into the creature and, with a choking gasp, it fell. He turned once again to the lights. His eyes glowed and his hand gripped the hilt of his weapon with a vengeful force.

Suddenly the room changed color again. The creature vanished in a puff of smoke. Darkness appeared, then changed to bright illumination. Red licking flames arose from the wall. Their writhing tongues reached up to the ceiling, and then burst toward Balzan in spurts of burning death.

He could feel the terrible heat, and sweat ran down his face. He swept his hand at the licking flames and then felt nothing. A crash like the beating of a thousand cymbals reverberated.

Balzan lifted both his arms in the air and his voice rang out loud and clear. "You are nothing, Zetar; all that you possess is from my mind."

Silence.

Then the flames fell tinkling to the floor, like shards of glass. The fire was suddenly stiff and cold, like the coagulated colors of the evil lights. Now Balzan advanced to the console. Vast confidence surged within him.

The pulsating lights danced across his face and he let his sword fall to the ground. He knew *now* the answers to all of his questions. The long-dead Zetarians had left their sentry to aid and enhance the life forms of the planet. The sentry could act only through a host and the brain of that host. Androth was the evil incarnate that the sentry had obeyed.

It could accomplish any task, perform any miracle, as long as stimuli were fed to it. Androth in his evil had used the machine to conquer races, condition them to fear, and, with the machine's restorative powers, combat aging in a bloodbath every ten years, known as the Feast of Zetar.

How many souls had been fed to the cold piece of metal before him? The thought sickened Balzan. The Zetarians in all their brilliance had failed to realize that such power in unscrupulous hands could only lead to a reign of terror and death. There were no mines to be worked. The slaves that were taken underground were fed to the sentry. After their intellect had been drained their bodies were destroyed.

Instead of utilizing the machine's great powers for good, Androth had succeeded in reprogramming the machine to be an instrument of evil—an evil that had to be destroyed.

All computers are ingrained with the self-destruct mechanism when their functions are no longer calibrated to perfection. All flaws are registered in memory circuits and, when detected, cancel its own system automatically.

Balzan spoke to the sentry that had stood for eons.

"Sentry, the great creators of your magnificence are all dead and as dust their memory clings. You who are the instrument of their perfection have strayed by your own imperfection. You 'have destroyed the concepts that created you. The creatures that you destroyed now weep along with the Zetarians for your errors. The host you chose has rendered you a flawed and evil force that can never again attain perfection. Your functions are over, Sentry. You have failed your creators and I now assume you as your host. As your host, I command you to destroy yourself. Without perfection you can no longer serve the Zetarians."

During what seemed an eternity of time a faint noise registered in the cavernous room. Then it rose louder. It was unmistakably the sound of the console. Now an unearthly roar grew.

Nearer and nearer.

The noise reached thunderous proportions.

The great wall flared and spat sparks and great sheets of flame. Abruptly, the lights faded and the cavern was dull and silent.

It burst forward for one last time in a brilliance that dazzled Balzan's eyes. The entire cave shook from the sound, the lights glowed with a painful radiance, a jewel lost in an image of stars. It flowed and sparkled like an arc light. Then the giant light crystals fell like melting icicles from its frame. They fell with a burned glassy glimmer. They tinkled to the floor of the cave and shattered into nothingness.

The lights of Zetar went black forever.

A distant rumble was heard overhead. The rock beneath Balzan's feet began to tremble. The rocks within began to grind. The stone walls began opening in zigzag cracks. Fragments of rock began hurtling through the air.

Balzan ran up the staircase to the passageway. The moment after he entered it the room behind him was buried by an avalanche of rocks.

He raced down the dimly lit corridor as the thunderous sounds of devastation followed him.

In the far corridor he saw the giant stalagmites crumble like ice shards. Rock collapsed and the floor began cracking in distorted jagged lines.

The sunlight, although a welcome sight, blinded the youth temporarily and he groped his way from the entrance to the safety of the trees beyond.

Turning, he saw the massive stone faces crack as if suddenly aged. Then in a labored movement they collapsed and crumbled into bits of strewn rock and debris.

The entire mountain seemed at first to shiver, then to tremble.

Then it exploded.

From a thousand positions within its massive body it burst into flames. It grew in force and fury. The mountain's core sucked in air with a giant gasp and added to the holocaust. It was a life within a life, a dirge to the millions of years of waiting, to the agony of deceit by a mortal being that had ended its attainment of perfection.

Balzan stood watching its death. Now, in the last slanting rays of the sun, the evening chill worked its way into his bones. He shivered, then turned and walked away from the burning mountain.

From his balcony in the palace, the Monitor observed the red haze in the distance. He possessed mixed feelings. One was sadness at the loss of his master, Androth. The second was jubilation that with Lenor's death he would be the new King of Manator. None could dispute his claim. It was the Forum's obligation to acknowledge his succession.

He summoned his servant to notify the priests of Zetar to join him in the throne room. He would first avail himself of the ritual of divinity, call for the mourning period of Androth, and later convene the Forum.

Outside the palace, in the city streets, pandemonium reigned. The Krell citizens, in panic at the awesome sight, were clamoring at the palace gates for consolation and protection.

The assembled Orathians and Corillians massed in the caves had begun their attack on the city. The garrison's prime duty was to guard the palace. The Monitor knew that Lord Emor would soon return and put down the revolt that now had reached Manator itself.

The priests bowed as the Monitor entered the great hall and took his seat upon Androth's throne.

The first priest knelt at the exalted one's feet and spoke in an exaggerated monotone.

"Great Monitor, the sphere of the fixed stars circles you favorably. The dragon who feeds its children its own blood, and the winged fauna which resuscitates in the flame, bless you."

The next priest fell beside the other and gave the sign of

obedience to the Monitor. "The gods have ordained you to save the people and to be the supreme master. You are the male of the sun, the heir of the fiery essence of gold. In your royal heart you and only you can exhaust the forces of evil. Your development in harmony with the gods will lead . . ."

The metallic clank of a gold caron striking the marble floor in front of the throne instantly stopped the priest's oratory.

The Monitor's eyes fell on Emor standing at the door with a look of amusement on his face. "You can dispense with your jesters, Monitor. Or should I call you King?"

A grimace danced across the Monitor's face but gradually was transformed into a smile. "Greetings, Lord Emor, your presence is a most welcome one indeed. The city needs your protective arm."

Emor approached the throne, removing his battle gloves and tossing them into the lap of a kneeling priest. "Get out," he rasped.

The priests shot a terrified glance to the Monitor, who gripped the sides of the throne in rage. Yet he nodded in assent and the men scurried through the door.

Emor poured a glass of wine from the table next to the throne and drank lustily. The Monitor remained silent. Finishing the wine, Emor hurled the goblet across the floor. "Did you really think that I would allow you to sit on the throne of Manator?"

The Monitor stiffened but held his anger in check. "What you feel about me is irrelevant, Lord Emor. With Princess Lenor's assassination and the master's death I am the successor to the throne."

"You are what I say you are, old man. And nothing more."

"Are you challenging my authority? If you are I think you will find the odds formidable against you!"

"Odds?" Emor laughed. "What odds? The only odds are how long you will remain alive. And that will be only as long as I choose."

The Monitor calmly lifted his baton and struck the metal disc beside him.

"A pity, Emor. You could have risen to even greater heights."

The counsel, amused, asked, "Who are you summoning? The elite guard?"

The Monitor nodded. "I have no alternative since you have threatened me. However, because of your past service I shall see that your death is a merciful one."

"Thank you. Only I'm afraid it shall be your death and not mine. And I will not make yours merciful. You have no elite guard. My fleet has entered the city. I and I alone command Manator."

The Monitor leaped to his feet and hissed at Emor. "You may challenge me, Emor, but you will not dare challenge the Forum."

The warrior counsel grabbed the old man by his robe and ripped him from the throne. He fell in a heap at its base.

"There is no Forum. There is only one semblance of order in the city now—mine. I did not return to save it for you. The rabble outside will fall because I have the power to defeat them. I—and only I."

The old man had no dignity left now. He nodded and his eyes became red and watery. "I cannot fight you, Emor. If you can save the city, you deserve the crown. I will place it on your brow myself and serve you as I served the master."

"If I allow you to serve me, old man," Emor sneered, "first I must destroy these carrion, then I shall return and we will talk of it. In the interim, remember that one attempt at any move to interfere with me, one gesture of treachery, and I will gut you on the spot."

The Monitor nodded weakly. He watched Emor walk defiantly out of the room. He labored to his feet and staggered to the throne.

He was tired now, defeated, his hopes dashed in an instant by the powerful warrior. His beloved Manator was under seige. He loved the city even though he knew its evil. But to cringe like a dog before Emor was unthinkable. He lifted himself up and drew his dagger from his cloak.

He knelt with it in his hands, and then with all his strength he plunged it into his breast. The pain was such that he cried out in agony, but the jeweled dagger went in, and then he fell upon it, driving it deeply into his body.

* * *

Jem led an assault wave upon the palace gates. He, who all of his young life had known only bloodshed and toil, now saw golden horizons. As he led his mass of revolting slaves, the results of their rebellion became clearer in his mind. The Orathians could do the same as the Krells. Soon they would be a force nothing could oppose.

In the frenzy of battle he heard the swelling timbre of his own greatness. The Krells would soon feel the lash, the emptiness of bellies bloated and hungry. All of the servitude he had endured would soon be transferred to the bowed heads of the Krells.

The first line of defense was weakening. A Krell warrior dropped to his knees and begged for mercy; but there was no mercy in the heart of Jem, as he raised his sword and drove it deep into the breast of the terrified Krell groveling before him.

The mass fought with such fury that in desperation the Krells fell back. They were about to enter the courtyard.

It was this scene that Balzan saw when he appeared. He saw the second line of defense armed and ready to slaughter the approaching slaves. Then, above the yells and curses of the battling men, there rose his screaming voice. "Fall back, it's a trap!"

His command fell on deaf ears as Jem and his army crashed through the gate and the horde swarmed out into the courtyard where the Krells awaited them. The palace gate closed behind them and they were caught like rats in a trap.

Emor, standing upon the battlements directing the engagement, gave the signal.

On all four sides of the trapped slaves stood the huge electronic spear guns that sent a projectile over thirty feet long at an explosive speed. The first one roared and ripped into the mass, scattering bodies in every direction. Then a second from the other side sent more slaves screaming in agony to the ground.

Jem thought and acted quickly in the emergency that had confronted them, taking advantage of the only means whereby he and his companions could be saved from the vengeance of the Krell warriors.

Throwing open the gates again he signaled and the men clambered out.

Emor gave his next command and the incendiary beams flashed. Over a hundred fell.

Balzan watched the carnage with clenched teeth, but was powerless to help. Jem turned and was appalled by the bloody shambles that met his astonished view. He stood dazed. He did not feel Balzan grasp his arm and lead him to cover. The slaves retreated in every direction. The seige was over. Lord Emor had saved the city. The slaves would regret their actions tenfold when he finished with them. At dawn his airships would lay devastation on the entire countryside. The blood that would run upon the land would be the blood of slaves.

Safe in the distance, Balzan and Jem watched the advancing Krells drive back their foes. Cursing and yelling, the Orathians and Corillians sought to climb over one another in their mad panic to escape. It was a gruesome sight from which Jem gladly turned at a signal from Balzan, following him to the caves where Tarlene would be waiting.

* * *

When Emor returned to the throne room he saw the figure lying in a pool of blood. When he turned him over the counsel saw that the face of the Monitor was fixed in a grimace or a grin.

One of his commanders rushed to his side. "Lord Emor, Balzan's forces have fled to the caves. There are only sporadic fires. Soon the city will be restored to order."

Emor's eyes flashed. "They are not Balzan's forces, commander. It is a rabble. One man cannot destroy Manator. But one can save it. Prepare my vessel and notify my fleet commanders. At dawn we shall attack."

Emor, King of the Krells. His image would take the place alongside that of Androth. His rule would be glorious. He had possessed foes who could withstand his military superiority. Manator had always educated a race of warriors, disciplined their courage, and trained them to use sophisticated weaponry.

The military art had been improved by Androth's genius and his miraculous inventions, which Emor fully intended to capitalize on. He commanded the two most powerful agents of nature, air and fire.

Mathematics, chemistry, and architecture had been applied to the service of war and conquest. His warriors possessed elaborate modes of attack and of defense. The revolting slaves would pay for a hundred years for their desecration of the memory of Androth. By nightfall Emor would have Balzan's head mounted on his flagship for all to see. Whenever the thought of revolt crossed their minds, they would remember the sight for many years.

He was so preoccupied by his dreams of glory that he did not notice the palace lights slowly dimming.

Chapter Sixteen

"Look!" Arc boisterously shouted at the mouth of the cave. "The city beacons have gone dark. The Krells are without their power source."

Balzan and Jem joined him at the entrance. It was as he had said. The Krell city lay wrapped in darkness.

Tarlene came unobtrusively up behind Balzan. "What does it mean?"

"It means the Krell butchers no longer have any weapons except the sword," Jem exclaimed jubilantly.

Balzan realized instantly what had transpired. With the computer's death the power source for the city had also perished. Auxiliary power that had been stored in battery form had powered their weapons during the battle. Tomorrow their airships would be useless. And with the slaves outnumbering the Krells fifty to one a victory was imminent.

"Hail to Balzan, our leader, who destroyed the mountain and with it brought our freedom."

The catacombs rang with cheers as Balzan colored and gestured humbly for them to cease. 'The battle is not won as yet, my friends. The Krells still possess fighting spirit and we must remember there are many Krell citizens that will be noncombatants. I'm sure we'll bring Emor to terms in short order."

"Terms?" Jem echoed. "What terms? We are not seeking terms. We are seeking vengeance for years of slavery and bloodshed. Every Krell that walks is to be slain. No quarter to any of them."

Balzan's eyes flashed as he grasped Jem's tunic. "You sound like the Krells you are fighting. What are you fighting for, Jem, freedom or power?"

Jem wrenched away from Balzan's grasp. "I have power, real power here in the strength of my arm. I'm not seeking peace with the Krells, I'm seeking their heads."

Balzan looked at the faces around him. Men and women who had known nothing but slavery all their lives and now stood on the threshold of changing their situation. He knew with a shudder that they all shared Jem's convictions.

"So now you are to be the masters, is that it?"

"Why not? We've been the dogs in the mud. Let us now stand with the stars."

Balzan made a mock bow. "To Jem, the new King of Manator."

The young Orathian's face hardened and he smashed his fist into Balzan's face, sending the youth staggering. Balzan wiped the blood from his lip and stared at his comrade, who stood ghastly white before him, clearly sorry for his sudden outburst of violence.

Jem's lips quivered and he groped for words. Then he turned and stalked from the cave.

Tarlene moved to Balzan and gently touched his arm. "You better go to him, Tarlene. Right now he needs the comforting," Balzan said.

Balzan slumped wearily upon a rock and saw the people staring at him. One of the Corillian children approached him and climbed into his lap. Balzan smiled down at the child and then spoke to the people.

"Victory can be yours and your freedom can be won. This can be accomplished by you."

"You are our leader, Balzan," Arc said. "We follow where you lead."

Balzan shrugged and his voice was soft, yet a touch of anger graced it. "Don't look for strong men as leaders. There aren't any. There are only people like yourself. They change, they die, they are weak like any other person. A united and strong race is the only lasting strength. Don't discount your enemies. They will always be there. The only thing that is important is to live."

"You cannot blame Jem, Balzan. He is a bitter young man with much hatred in him."

"I don't, Arc. I also wish to destroy Krells, but only the Krells who cannot see the futility of war. I will be fighting alongside you tomorrow and when we are victorious we can afford to be merciful. The Krells do not have to be eliminated to insure success."

"You speak so strangely, Balzan. I am not sure I understand your words."

"The Krells were dominated by Androth. He used an alien culture to conquer and enslave you. His orders, his rule, moved the Krell machine. Now he is destroyed and with him the power that kept you as slaves. Victory is one thing. But to place Orathian and Corillian as new masters seems to me a poor cause for war. Why not build together a new and greater world? That is a worthy and noble venture."

Jem and Tarlene returned. Jem extended his hand. "Forgive me, Balzan."

The youth grasped it warmly.

"I still follow you and am ready to carry out your orders."

Balzan turned to his followers. "First we immobilize their airships which could still have auxiliary power left. Then we take the palace. Afterward we present our demands to the Krell leaders."

At dawn the slaves had encircled the city. Soon afterward they began their attack, with the blowing of horns and the shouting of people now maddened beyond endurance by the yoke of servitude.

Emor dispatched fifty cohorts who charged the rebels. The Corillians, seeing the charging Krells, did not try to meet them but, opening their ranks, let them through and then closed the circle and killed all of them.

After that Balzan and the Orathians came up from the other entrance to the city. The Krells, their numbers growing fewer and fewer, fought and died in vain.

As the day wore on only a hundred warriors still clustered about Emor's palace stronghold.

The Krells formed a tightly packed ring and stood leaning on their hacked and bloody swords for support, watching the red sun begin to sink on the horizon.

For many of them that dying sun was an omen of their own death and that of the Krell empire.

From the tower Emor watched all this. His crew stood at alert in his airship. There was enough auxiliary power left to carry him over the sea and out of reach of the slaves. If necessary he would journey to the Mork province and regroup his forces.

Now only the elite guard stood between him and the mob below. Emor was sumptuously dressed in a gold tunic and gold trappings. He wore his sword and caron. A hurled javelin creased his helmet and he fell to the floor. He staggered up, his face contorted into a look compounded of fear and hatred, pride and anger.

Balzan was one level below him, slashing with his comrades through the last line of defense. He reached the roof. In the wash of light he saw the gold tunic in the twin moons' brilliance. The emblem was unmistakable—it was Emor. The flagship *Zetar*'s motors hummed in readiness for a speedy departure.

Only a handful of the elite guard stood between Balzan and the Krell counsel.

Balzan unsnapped his therb and uncoiled its full length.

Some of the last vestiges of habitual unthinking pride clung to Emor and he looked over at the youth brandishing the strange weapon. With a motion of his sword he sent two Krells charging Balzan.

The therb cracked.

The poison barbs tore into the lead Krell's neck and he collapsed, screaming in agony. The second hesitated, then valiantly charged. Balzan's aim was flawless and the barbs ripped into the Krell's face, sending him spiraling off the tower roof to plunge into the sea below.

"Surrender, Emor, and the killing will cease," Balzan shouted.

The counsel stared at him with eyes in which an agony had been born. Then he spun away and clamored up the ladder and roared at two warriors who were guarding the mooring lines. "Cast off!"

Balzan struck one warrior in the back. But even in his death agony the soldier, in blind loyalty, severed the line. The other Krell split the last line and leaped to the rail clinging with desperation as the giant airship ponderously began rising into the air.

Balzan replaced his therb and bolted for the swinging mooring lines. He leaped in the air and grasped the leather line. A Krell above him drew his sword to sever it and Balzan, swinging like a pendulum, swung out and grasped a chain on the hull. Clinging precariously to this new hold, he slowly drew himself upward until he could grasp the rail. The ship gained altitude and steered on a course over the sea. Balzan clung to the rail and the Krell slashed at him from above. The ship lurched and the man went off balance. Balzan seized his wrist and yanked and the Krell shot downward through the air, screaming. Balzan climbed over the rail onto the deck and before he could draw his sword, was attacked by another warrior. He sidestepped the blade that swished harmlessly in the air over his head. Then he moved in with both feet planted and smashed his fist into the face. The blow sent the Krell backward over the rail into the blackness below.

As the ship gained altitude it veered unsteadily, buffeted by the sudden wind at this height and from the boarding and landing tackle trailing beneath the keel. The pilot struggled with the stabilizer and the ship maneuvered sluggishly.

Balzan drew his sword and entered the control room. Two Krells turned to meet him. He dodged them easily as they attacked. Balzan's lunge found its mark in the lead Krell's throat, the cruel steel head of the Kharnite sword then smashed bloodily into the chest of the other.

The pilot turned and reached for his sword just as Balzan plunged his blade in the pilot, who doubled up and fell sideways.

Balzan went to the steering panel and his eyes darted over the unfamiliar instruments. Behind him he heard the door open and Emor stood in its archway, his sword gleaming almost as bright as his eyes.

"Balzan," he sneered.

The young human stood eye to eye with the Krell commander. "Yes, Emor—your executioner."

The airship, without the hands of a pilot, slowly dipped and began descending. Balzan was sent lurching toward Emor.

The Krell brought his sword down in an arc that missed Balzan but smashed into the glass cylinders that held the vessel's fuel. There was a spark and then small fingers of fire darted out and followed the spilled liquid to the control panel.

Balzan parried Emor's next blow, but with his free hand the Krell smashed his fist into the youth's head.

Balzan was thrown into the wall and Emor was upon him instantly. The youth slashed out and knocked the blade from the Krell's hand. Emor then grasped Balzan's sword wrist and they wrestled to the floor. The fuel upon the instrument panel ignited and burst into more flames. Soon dense smoke filled the cabin.

The two men locked in combat smashed through the door to the deck. There was a massive short circuit in the primary power and an explosion ripped the control room. The blast sent both men sprawling. Emor almost toppled over the railing from its force.

Now the ship was descending at a more rapid pace. Its course was the mountain that lay dead ahead. Balzan struggled to his feet. Emor drew his caron and lashed out at the youth, grazing his head and sending him to the deck. As he attempted to rise Emor kicked him in the chest.

The surge of uncontrolled fire shot far out from the control room and was eating its way over the bridge to the huge gas-filled balloon above. When the flames reached the gas, the result would be immediate and catastrophic.

Emor swung his caron again. Balzan reached out and grabbed his arm. His muscles strained and his face, reflected in the flame, was the face of blind fury. The applied pressure forced the Krell to open his hand and drop the weapon.

Balzan backhanded him, then brought the same hand back balled into a fist and crushed the Krell's nose in a savage blow.

The ship was an inferno and was skimming not more than fifty feet above the water. Balzan saw the collision course it was heading on and leaped over the rail into the sea below.

The ship, like a horizontal burning candle, wove and dipped toward the wall of rock ahead.

Emor only had time to rise to his feet before his life ended in a fiery holocaust.

The impact of the ship striking the mountain lit up the night in a brilliant burst of orange and crimson. Its explosive power was unbelievable. The force and fury of the blast ripped giant pieces of rock from the mountain's face and hurled them like juggernauts into the sky.

As Balzan reached shore, thunder was grumbling and the wind was building. He looked over his shoulder at the black and red glow that moments before had been the flagship *Zetar*. He shook his head and wiped the back of his hand wearily across his forehead. Then he trudged back toward the city.

The sight that greeted Balzan upon his return in the first rays of dawn was not pleasant.

Jem had not been idle during the night. Orathians were leading Krell women and children tied by cords like beasts. He saw Jem sitting on a makeshift throne with Krell men before him. He had forced what looked like over twenty of them to kneel. At his signal a band of Corillians beheaded every one of them.

But what sickened Balzan the most was the sight of Tarlene sitting next to her brother. She was smiling and applauding Jem's actions. It was a metamorphosis that staggered Balzan's senses. A day before she had been the tender, caring, loving Tarlene who had implored him to leave and start life anew with her. Now she resembled the Krell Princess Lenor. It was almost as if she were her successor.

Balzan advanced toward the gathering, his brain in a fever, his rage gathering like a storm. He stopped when he saw Arc sitting alone, holding his head in his hands.

"Arc," Balzan rasped.

The Corillian looked up into Balzan's eyes and merely shook his head. "Look about you, Balzan. See how merciful we are. I do not know any of these creatures I called comrade. All I see now are Krells with a different skin."

Jem sighted Balzan and cheered his name. "Balzan, our leader, come see the dogs that we have conquered grovel for their worthless lives."

Seeing Balzan, Tarlene broke into a wide smile and raced to him with outstretched arms.

She reached for him and he viciously slammed her to the ground. He turned to Jem.

"You filth! I should have known you for a lying dog."

But Jem turned to him pale-faced and replied, "Save your hatred for the Krells, Balzan. You can either stand in glory with us or fall. You choose."

Tarlene scampered to him, her eyes pleading. "Jem has to rid the people of these monsters. Don't you realize that the city is ours, Balzan? We are the power now and they are the slaves. And you are the greatest of all of us. Don't reject the ones who love you."

Balzan looked at the woman before him as if she were not even there. Any love that he had felt for her had been ripped from his heart as surely as a knife would have done.

141

He saw Jem back toward his men. Balzan approached him. All kindliness and tolerance deserted him.

An old Krell priest was lying upon the ground. Balzan tore a water pouch from a Corillian and offered the old man water.

Immediately Jem sprang forward, his face contorted in fury at Balzan's actions. Jem kicked the pouch from Balzan's hands and shouted, "I want this Krell dead, Balzan."

Balzan turned to Jem and spat out his words. "Give him water, Jem, or I will kill you right now."

Jem looked around at his followers. They were cowering away from the young human whom they regarded as a god.

"Give him water," Balzan roared.

As Jem shrank back at this blaze of anger, the priest, his cracked lips scarcely damp, looked up at Balzan with tears in his eyes.

For a moment Jem held Balzan's gaze, then with his composure regained he cried out in a rising voice, "Our merciful Balzan wishes to help the priest. Very well."

Jem knelt and lifted the old priest's head up. Then, in a horrible movement, brought out his dagger and slashed the old man's throat.

Balzan in a lightning move drew his sword and slashed off Jem's arm in a single stroke. Jem rolled on the ground screaming in terror. Not one man moved to aid him.

Balzan looked upon them and fought back the sob that was racking his body. He turned to the crowd. "Here is your new king. You all deserve him."

Balzan walked away from the people he had called family. As he walked he knew their end was assured, because no Orathian or Corillian could ever trust the other again.

With the Krells destroyed, they had spawned an even greater enemy.

Themselves.

Epilogue

The thin gold and emerald flecks of the twin moons floated slowly downward and reflected on the dark surface of the waters. The stars beyond the sky seemed to come nearer to the two men who sat upon the beach gazing outward into the sea.

The glitter of the stars and moons gave a luster to the waves that pounded the shore and the cragged rocks. The sea breeze brought the breath of the water itself to them. The perfume of it brought the gift of freshness and solace.

"Where will you go?" Arc asked softly.

Balzan smiled without looking at him. "It's a big world, Arc. I'll find my place in it somewhere."

Arc stared at him, his features tightening into something he was beginning to recognize as a shell erected by a man who was lost and disappointed.

"You cared for both Tarlene and Jem very much, didn't you?"

Arc had touched a part of him which even his indifference at that moment could not hide.

His eyes changed oddly, grew thoughtful and sad. He leaned back and turned and looked over the entire landscape, the sea, then across toward the mountains.

"Yes, I did care," he answered.

"Do you have to leave?"

"Yes," he answered.

"But where, Balzan?"

Once again his gaze swept the shoreline. "Where my nose leads me." He smiled at Arc, "You have to remember we are different."

"Tell me," said Arc.

"You are a Corillian. I'm a human being from another

world, a world I shall never see. But I possess the inner feelings of my race and probably always will."

"Feelings?"

"I should say instinct. The instinct that causes humans to band together in the face of danger is based on bonds of affection. It's a response that grows out of the affection between parents and children. But your race does not know that kind of affection."

"In a sense we do, Balzan. I feel a great kinship for you."

"And I for you as well, Arc, but it's different. And no other Corillian or Orathian could understand it."

Arc's brow wrinkled.

"The only love you have is admiration, a transitory love without lasting. Do you understand?" Balzan asked.

Arc shook his head.

"No matter. It's your world, Arc. It's my prison."

Balzan got to his feet and extended his hand to the Corillian.

"Peace and happiness, Arc."

"And to you also, Balzan of Endore."

With a burst of sudden emotion Arc embraced Balzan and nodded. "I will miss you, comrade."

Arc watched him as he walked away. A water pouch was slung over one shoulder. He heard Balzan whistle some lilting melody. The world was wide and he would lose himself in it.

Arc shouted, "Good luck."

But Balzan did not hear him.

A wind fanned Balzan's face as he walked and it refreshed him. The clouds had lifted higher with the wind, and on the highest farthest fold of the pinnacles nestled between the two moons lay another unknown region. Perhaps it was a valley with gentle rain and gentle folk.

Wherever he trod on this strange planet Balzan knew he could always look forward to experiences that were unique.

For he was unique himself. One of a kind.

The unknown once again lay ahead of him.

Behind him lay the city.

Balzan did not look back.